MAMA'S BOY BEHIND BARS

MAMA'S BOY

BEHIND BARS

Book*hug Press
Toronto, 2019
Literature in Translation Series

FIRST ENGLISH EDITION

Published originally under the title *La bête et sa cage* © 2016, Les Éditions Internationales
Alain Stanké, Montreal, Canada
English translation copyright © 2019 by J.C. Sutcliffe

The production of this book was made possible through the generous assistance of the Canada
Council for the Arts and the Ontario Arts Council. Book*hug also acknowledges the support
of the Government of Canada through the Canada Book Fund and the Government of Ontario
through the Ontario Book Publishing Tax Credit and the Ontario Book Fund.

We acknowledge the financial support of the Government of Canada through the National
Translation Program for Book Publishing, an initiative of the Roadmap for Canada's Official
Languages 2013-2018: Education, Immigration, Communities, for our translation activities.

Book*hug Press acknowledges the land on which it operates. For thousands of years it has
been the traditional land of the Huron-Wendat, the Seneca, and most recently, the Mississaugas
of the Credit River. Today, this meeting place is still the home to many Indigenous people from
across Turtle Island, and we are grateful to have the opportunity to work on this land.

Library and Archives Canada Cataloguing in Publication

Title: Mama's boy behind bars / David Goudreault ; translated by JC Sutcliffe.
Other titles: Bête et sa cage. English
Names: Goudreault, David, author. | Sutcliffe, J. C., translator.
Series: Literature in translation series.
Description: First English edition. | Series statement: Literature in translation series |
Translation of: La bête et sa cage.
Identifiers: Canadiana (print) 20190118059 | Canadiana (ebook) 20190118091
ISBN 9781771664851 (softcover) | ISBN 9781771664868 (HTML)
ISBN 9781771664875 (PDF) | ISBN 9781771664882 (Kindle)
Classification: LCC PS8613.O825 B4813 2019 | DDC C843/.6—dc23

PRINTED IN CANADA

For perpetuity

PROLOGUE

I've killed two people now. I'm a serial killer. So maybe a body count of two isn't exactly serial, but it's a start. I'm still young. Who knows where opportunity might lead me? Opportunity makes the thief, or the murderer, or even the pastry chef. It's well documented.

For the last four days, my world has been shrunk down to the size of an isolation cell. My lawyer's just been by to bring me paper and pencils. He claims it'll help me kill time and might come in useful to us at the trial. Apparently my writing's of great interest to the legal guys and all manner of specialists. I seriously don't know what they get out of it, but my lawyer, all dressed up in his Sunday best, swears it'll be psychiatrist catnip.

Last time I murdered someone, I wrote down the whole story. The experts took inspiration from it when they wrote up their psychological reports. Which means that reports using my own sentences played their part in decisions about my sentence.

They said my story was disarmingly transparent and frank. It should have worked in my favour. Seems the verdict was that I have minimal capacity for introspection even though I express myself richly. That's because of all my studies in nothing whatsoever. I'm self-taught from head to toe. At the trial I swaggered about, feeling pretty proud of myself.

But then they started listing off a whole string of diagnoses: dysphasia, flexibility, and adaptation issues that might point to autism, and anti-social and narcissistic personality disorders. The specialists teamed up to make me out to be a complex psychopath, even though I was so young. That was less flattering.

I got sixteen years in the slammer. Clang! They told me it could have been worse. It'll be worse this time, for sure, now I've reoffended. I might never know freedom again. But freedom's all in your head. And I have a huge skull.

As I wait for them to finish their inquiry and decide what degree of murder I'm going down for, I'm stewing in isolation, so I might as well write.

I'll tell the truth, the whole truth, and nothing but my truth. This manuscript may be submitted to the judge, the jury, the psychiatric experts, and a publisher. Odds are it'll be a long trial and a good book.

1

JUSTICE

When it comes to sodomy, I'm a passive kind of guy; I mostly just wait for it to be over. When I ended up in prison, I soon realized this would be the best attitude to adopt. Trying to argue only turned my attacker on. And if I wasn't getting a kick out of it, I certainly wasn't going to give him one.

Society is so prejudiced about people who take it up the ass. But we're not doing anything wrong. The ones doing the ass-fucking are the ones getting their hands dirty. Or other parts of their anatomy. Especially in the kind of sexual assaults I've been subjected to since my first few hours in prison. But the social prejudice weighs heavily on the back of the person being taken up the ass. I never wanted to be that person, and I've never done anything to make it happen. Being fucked up the ass is bad for a person's self-esteem. But nobody ever criticizes the person doing the fucking. It's a deep injustice. I don't think we'll be seeing groups standing up for buggered people any time soon. Sad.

The giant sodomizing me went by the pseudonym of Butterfly. Don't let his delicate nickname fool you. He got it from his first conviction: he blinded his girlfriend with a butterfly knife.

He caught her looking at photos of an ex. Butterfly didn't appreciate that kind of nostalgia. The broad survived, minus an eye.

So for the last six months, this brute Butterfly has been working hard to increase my sphincter flexibility. It's been tough, but you can get used to anything, especially if it goes on for long enough. The butterfly in question needed to make out with me every day. Over time, it became irritating but tolerable. For the body, anyway. The head never gets used to being raped.

Optimists like to say that things could always be worse. If Butterfly hadn't chosen me for his boo, I wouldn't have benefited from his protection. Every other prisoner in the joint would have had a claim on my ass. And Butterfly was a high-up dude in Big Dick's gang. So even if his libido was suffering from morbid obesity, and even if he used to make me wax my crack and balls, just by being under his command, I too, by extension, was a little bit part of the gang. I aspired, in some nearish future, to establish professional rather than sexual relations.

I should explain that in prison it's not homosexuality. It's simply managing the surplus testosterone in a closed circuit—a very complicated intermittent circuit. Unless you have a history of it before you get here. And even among back-door connoisseurs, there's a whole spectrum of differences. There are gays, queers, fairies, and homosexuals. You shouldn't lump them all together, even though they sometimes overlap. But I'm none of those things. I'm just a virile hetero in an unfortunate position. Even though he's bald, Butterfly is also a very virile hetero, but after four years in the slammer he's gay for the stay.

Under Butterfly's protection I had nothing to fear—except him. Which was plenty. People who say that those who bark don't bite are wrong. Butterfly barked and bit constantly. His six-foot frame was like the body of a Rottweiler crossed with the personality of a vicious chihuahua. He yelled and screamed and yelled, and if he got a chance to bite a foot, he'd take off with the calf too. I don't think he ever had a mother: he was the offspring of a Viking chief and an Ostrogoth blacksmith. Basically he was a caricature of a monster, the kind that's a dime a dollar in every prison. He'd blown a fuse once, and now he had a screw loose. One time I saw him smash an inmate's head into a mirror for brushing his teeth too slowly. He wasn't even in his way; Butterfly never brushes his teeth.

I got a taste of his medicine the first time I dared reject him. In vain did I scream, argue, and remind him that I'd just killed a defenceless old lady: he was unimpressed. And he showed me just how unimpressed with a quick head-butt to the jaw. I'm still waiting for dentures; the state should be buying me some new teeth soon. That's one of the advantages of being a social pariah: free dental.

You can't tell from the writing on the page, but since it happened, I now whistle more than I speak. I try to articulate and stop the air getting through. It's hard to establish a gangster reputation with a voice full of air. Threats don't have the same edge when they're whistled. *I'm going to flaughter you, you piefe of fffit!* See what I mean?

The most spectacular thing about Butterfly's body is his tattoos. His skin is covered with them. Dragons, whores, tribal symbols, skulls. Even on his face. Barbed wire climbs his neck up to his eyebrows and around his eyes. And, like a trinity of cherries on a sundae, three tears mark the corner of his right eye, one for each murder.

I don't have any confidence or any tattoos. When I've

covered my body with enough messages, I'll be less afraid of asserting myself. But I won't need to, then; my skin will speak for me. I'll be able to expand my self-esteem and my ambitions. I know I'm a criminal genius, and maybe even a genius full stop. You can feel these things. I feel strongly. And I'm not just being pretentious—I'm not pretending anything, I'm asserting!

One day I'll flaunt both my successes and my tattoos in people's faces. I'll be covered in barbed wire, but I'll throw some eagles and knights in the mix too. On my back, there'll be bullet holes around a big samurai armed with a Japanese katana. That's to scare off any bastards who want to attack me from behind.

And between my thumb and my index finger, the prisoner's star will twinkle. This symbol is only for the true, the unrepentant. People who've done hard time in a real max-security institution, not a nice little vacation in some local jail. Sentences of less than two years are for limp dicks. If you're going to do time, you might as well do it properly.

You can't judge by the ceremonial jewels; bling is pretty enough, but with a tattoo you're inked for life. You can take the ring off the guy, but you can't take the guy off his dragon. A tattooed guy is always more dangerous. It's like a constant reminder: be worthy of your balls, be a man.

Anyway, I'd planned to get several tattoos before my next murder. I was lucky, blocks with a needle artist on hand are rare. Especially in the "Wing for Protecting Inmates with Mental Health Problems." Man, civil servants really know how to choose a good name.

And that wasn't fair either, locking me up with the crazies instead of letting me network in the normal sections. My lawyer screwed up: they wouldn't recognize me as crazy in court, but then they shoved me in the ding wing! Our justice system is more contradictory than the emotions of a histrionic teenager menstruating at full moon. Why was I in prison instead of seeing a psychiatrist? Why was so-and-so in psychiatry while his accomplice was in prison? Why was Pedo in jail instead of in therapy? And if they're so eager to separate out the mentally ill from the criminals, why is there a special loony section in every prison in the country? They're trying to mess with our heads: those fuckers are more dangerous than we are.

Justice is an exact science that gets it wrong every time.

And who gets to define mentally ill, anyway? Who exactly is this normal person who can claim to be sound of mind? Our entire society's infected. On a small scale, I'm mentally ill, but if you take a wider perspective, I become a social symptom. I'm the forbidden fruit of your tree that's rotten to its roots.

But enough with the ethics. I've got to see out a sixteen-year sentence with people who aren't right in the head. But I'm pretty sure I'll only do two-thirds, maybe less. I've been doing all the therapeutic activities, and I'm always licking my correctional officer's boots. I'll get my sentence reduced. And anyway, I've got a plan for the future: when I get out, I'm going to give conferences and personal-growth workshops. My correctional officer doesn't think there'll be that much demand for someone like me. But she can't dampen my enthusiasm. People eat up stories of resilience with all the twists and turns, and journalists adore them. People love role models, especially the beaten-up models who've been chewed up and spat out by the system. It makes the taxpayers feel safe. I can give them their money's worth.

Prisons look depressing, both outside and inside. The architecture is almost as ugly and austere as a high school building. It's all beige-painted cement, or even just raw concrete. And everywhere you look, there are armoured doors with tiny grilled windows to let a trickle of light in.

Our section starts at the observation box next to the office where guards meet prisoners to discuss their cases. The box is a central control post from where the guard can see two sections at a time. He's responsible for unlocking the cell-block doors and also monitors the guards on the ground. You never know who's inside because the guard on duty is hidden behind a two-way mirror. Naturally we feel obliged to pick our teeth or noses in front of this mirror.

Adjacent to this famous observation box is the prison guards' office. *Office* is maybe not the right word. It's the place where the guards meet inmates one-on-one, so they haven't missed a trick, security-wise. It's a cramped room, with a big table with only a phone, some files, and a panic button. Two plastic chairs. And the rehabilitation of the worst criminals in Quebec takes place in this minimalist decor. What a charming mausoleum.

The office and the guard room are opposite the common area where the only furniture is four cement tables, each surrounded by four benches, just like at McDonalds. There's the television too, of course, which is absolutely essential. This living space is surrounded by our cells, three on each side. Two inmates to a cell, in the vast majority of cases.

The way we were paired up in cells wasn't just chance. These things have a way of working out, as people who actually work out say. I was in a cell with Philippe the Filipino, although Butterfly also spent way too much time there. Officially, the bodyguard who was throwing himself at my body shared his cell with Big Dick, the top boss of the whole place. Denis lived with Giuseppe. Colossus with Louis-Honoré. Timoune with Gilbert. And Pedo lived alone, for his own safety.

You shouldn't get attached to these characters; several of them will disappear during the course of our journey. Murders happen so quickly.

I shared a cell with the tattooer, which would end up having major consequences. For an immigrant from a poor country, he was pretty talented. He hadn't even studied art on his poverty-stricken island. He was Filipino, even though he'd lost all his exoticness and spoke with a Laval accent. He was Filipino so we called him Philippe. It wasn't the name his mother gave him, but it was more practical that way. His real name was unpronounceable, and Philippe the Filipino has a nice ring.

Our wing also houses an Italian. A real live Italian, with greasy black hair and everything, but he had nothing to do with the Mafia. How fucked up is that? An Italian without connections is worth even less than a Filipino. If I'd been lucky enough to be Italian, I'd have proved myself long ago: killed for the family, bled on a photo of the Virgin, taken the oath, and I'd be all in. I'd have *Cossa Notra* tattooed over my heart and a beautiful plump little mamma mia in the kitchen. Murder and spaghetti on tap. And to top it all off, this Italian with no contacts was called Giuseppe even though he was only twenty-seven. You're only allowed to call yourself Giuseppe if you're over seventy.

Giuseppe and Philippe were in the same boat. Or the same raft, to be more accurate. They were vulnerable mercenaries caught between two gangs. A pair of innocents in survival mode, waiting to be recruited, transferred, or assassinated. The law of the streets is hard inside. The summer looked like it was shaping up to be a hot one, especially for we who have to sail in troubled waters.

On one side there was Big Dick the all-powerful, with Butterfly and Denis under him. He'd got the nickname Big Dick when he used to work with Mom. Not Mom Boucher, Mom Paquette. Criminals are usually creative types, but there's a definite preference for certain pseudonyms: Kid, Baby, Fingers, Little, Scars, Tiny, Tony, and Mom, for example. Big Dick is less common. His full name was Great Big Dick. He was a major figure in the biker wars, in the pay of the Italians. His detractors liked to call him Big Fat Dick to diss him.

Big Dick had a head where his heart should be. Using this awesome calculator, each one of his actions had a specific aim. He was a boss, it goes without saying. And, like me, he wasn't supposed to be in a section with brain-damaged people.

The hierarchy goes like this: Big Dick at the top, Denis on his right, Butterfly on the executive committee, and then me, unofficially, underneath Butterfly. Rather too often for my liking. Our gang of Aryan Brotherhood wannabes was in charge of all trafficking in drugs and cellphones. Big Dick, our chief, derived some of his power from my lover's physical strength, as well as from his amazing contacts both inside and outside the prison walls. While he was doing time, he'd left his business affairs in the east of the city in the hands of some real genuine Mafia Italians. He also had a corrupt correctional officer in his pocket, Tony, who kept him up-to-date with everything going on inside. Under his command, the white guys called the shots.

Facing off against us were the black guys, all innocent-looking. Big Dick tolerated Colossus and his henchmen, Louis-Honoré and Timoune, who were Haitians. Colossus liked to be precise, so he claimed to be from Réunion, which is a major city in the Haitian archipelago. These guys were skilled at procurement. Incidentally, Butterfly had negotiated exclusive access to my ass through Colossus. The black guys also specialized in contracts: beatings and murders. Demand was low at the time. In a wing with only eleven inmates, you soon reach equilibrium.

The black guys also had a stranglehold on the tattooing profits. They provided the ink, made up of oil and cigarette ash when pens were in short supply, as well as the motor and the guitar strings to pound the skin. You had to go through them if you wanted to get inked by Philippe. Butterfly had negotiated a good price for the swastika on his shoulder blade.

I'm into black guys who like hip hop. I'd have loved to be in the black guys' gang, but I was told in no uncertain terms that I had to stick with my own race. No chance of appeal.

It sucks big-time, since I've always dreamed of rapping with black guys. I've always felt close to them, I have rhythm in my blood. My entire existence becomes meaningful when I listen to rap. I write it too, I'm still working on my first album. You won't have heard anything like it; it's more unique than a Wayne Gretzky rookie card signed by Mario Lemieux with his own blood. With my major ex-con cred, I'll totally storm the charts.

Like Timoune and Louis-Honoré, I shaved my head. It made me look less ginger and it was more practical in fights. Colossus had no need for any such capillary prevention: he let his long dreads grow down to the middle of his back. Nobody would have dared start anything with him; his father had taken charge of his education by making him referee dogfights. That's where he got all his scars—and his annoying habit of biting people in the face.

Even if I couldn't make friends with the black guys, I stayed hip hop in my soul. Anyway, hip hop isn't even that black anymore. It was taken away from black people, like blues, jazz, soul, bebop, rock and roll, funk, disco, reggae, and so on and so on. White people have always stolen black music. But don't forget, the best rappers in the world are Eminem, the Beastie

Boys and Vanilla Ice, all little white guys. I didn't need a black band to become a good rap group or make a solo career. All I needed was that hip hop in my soul.

From Wu-Tang to Ku Klux, it's always the same thing—people's need for a clan. Same same but different, the Chinese would say. But although the gangs worked with each other on occasion, the tension in our section was palpable. It might explode at any moment. Underneath the debts, the swindles, the aggressions, and the psychiatric symptoms simmered a soup of troubles. If you lock eleven psychopaths up in five square metres, you can hardly expect them to start a knitting club.

Orbiting around these two clans who controlled the immigrants and me were two civilians: Gilbert and Pedo. Gilbert the hooch guy and Pedo, just Pedo. Pedo was overmedicated, ugly, and despised; no gang wanted him in its ranks. It was natural selection, he isolated himself, anyway.

As for Gilbert, he kept his independence thanks to his talent as a brewer. This makeshift alchemist produced the best artisanal alcohol made in any Canadian prison. Obviously, there aren't many official tastings, so it's easy to claim the title. But whatever, Gilbert had the recipe and the power to negotiate prices with his friends or to piss in his enemies' rations. This allowed him to remain a free agent.

This whole hooch deal used to give me some problems. I was okay with contributing to production with my oranges, apples, and tomatoes so I could get my share. But I refused to hand over my bread. I kept that for the birds I was taming in a corner of the yard. They were mourning doves. Rhoooo rhooooo hoooo. I love their song and I need contact with animals. I had to dodge the brewer's surveillance as well as that of the two rival clans, united in their desire to have the maximum possible moonshine.

I prefer drugs, even if alcohol is a drug like all the others, and hardly any more dangerous and debilitating. My withdrawal from both was hard. My consumption had dropped radically since I'd been in prison. So, it was yes to the moonshine and yes to any medication that could go up my nose. Prison is no place to be fussy. That was the hardest thing to adapt to. I needed to get high, it was a matter of life or death. I was prepared to do anything. It took some effort, getting fucked enough to not give a fuck.

I stole, did some extras, and tracked down a little line here, a puff there. There's no shame in it; the quest for drugs is no less noble than the quest for the Holy Grail.

And then, of course, there was the third gang operating in our wing, the only one with the right to wear colours: the correctional officers, or guards, or you-big-dirty-dog-fucker-when-I-get-out-of-here-I'm-gonna-kill-your-whole-family, depending on your mood. They're nice enough dropouts who used to dream of being in the police. Now they've got the grey uniform—no gun, no big paycheque, no social status, but at least they have the inmates, already locked up, to watch over.

In addition to the guard in the box, there were six that alternated in our particular wing, the loony wing. Six brave civil servants down on the floor with the beasts. Four men and two women. One obese old auntie assisted by a facially challenged young woman. People say beauty's on the inside, but it certainly wasn't inside in that prison! So there was one unusable woman and one ugly young woman, but you make do. But I didn't get bored stiff masturbating over her. Edith, my darling, my unforgettable, my own special officer. Edith. She must have been hit on more during one shift in the prison than during a night out clubbing. It's therapeutic for ugly women to work in a prison.

So all the characters are in place. I'll knock one off along the way. Will this or that one die or not? The suspense! I hope to have the time to write the whole story before my summons. It will do me good to get back to the courtroom, take a few rides in the paddy wagon, and enjoy the air conditioning. It'll break the routine even if it doesn't break my chains.

You get used to being imprisoned. Even being overcrowded with the worst specimens of humanity. But being reminded thirty times a day, at every locked door, at every checkpoint, at every light's out—it all gets pretty intense and heavy, like Justice doesn't even care about the scales anymore. And during a heat wave, cooped up with guys who are sweaty, stinky, and can't even be bothered to move their irritable carcasses, time passes slowly. Prison's hard. Even harder than Butterfly.

2

SHARING

My mother wrote to me. She wrote a long letter of excuses, full of love and promises. She went on at length about all the wounds in her soul, the burns in her mother's heart, her continuous floods of tears. Every sentence was filled with regret at being separated from me, for not having known how to love me or how to help me when she could. She signed off with lots of capital Xs for kisses and some hearts.

At least, that's what I imagined. But the only letter I'd had in six months was held up by the management. My imbecile lawyer, believing I was in strict isolation, had neglected to get me to fill in the forms for receiving mail. And then when a personal letter showed up, which was obviously from my mother, it had to wait for a bureaucrat to get his ass in gear.

All I could do was wait, dream hard, and hope big.

Big Dick was skinny. But he was well connected. No need for muscles when you're the brains of the business. Not even any need for tattoos, in his case. He carried himself with an authority full of charisma and experience. He got sent down for dealing. Big dealing, big sentence.

Big Dick was the only guy in our section who hadn't been locked up for violent crime. But rumour had it he'd done plenty, all for the Italians. Even if he was old-stock Quebec from way back. You haven't got many options if you're not into motorbikes, you don't want to join a gang, and you specialize in anything that makes money. Especially since the Dubois family, the Provençals and Montreal's other great crime families aren't spawning too many new mini-Mafiosi. What a loss of beautiful traditions.

So he was a Cossa Notra subcontractor, this big, skinny guy in his fifties, grizzled and starting to bald, and with this crazy leopard's eye. I can't think of another way to describe it, it was the look of a wildcat ready to pounce. It was easy for him to become the boss of the wing, especially in a protected area like ours. Unlike me, he didn't want to be with the regular inmates in the general population. There were too many bikers in the other sections—dangerous for a Mafia associate like him. And the crazies get out of working, which is a major advantage for someone who refuses to enrich the state in return for poverty wages.

I dreamed of being in his shoes. Even in the slammer, with limited power, being the boss isn't nothing. Especially the boss of a band of mentally ill murderers. If you're going to be leader of the herd, you should avoid being leader of a herd of sheep. As for me, I wanted to be in the place of the big boss, the alpha male who controls the betas. I'd rather reign over three men inside than be three times nothing outside.

Big Dick never spoke to me. He only ever spoke to his two lieutenants: his right-hand man, Denis, and Butterfly, his henchman. The latter was the one I had to impress to get close to the boss. For the time being, he was raping me more than he was softening toward me, but I had a plan for reversing that ratio.

Sooner or later I was going to replace him in the hierarchy and maybe even become his boss. From that moment on he would no longer be a threat. Henchmen can be good right-hand men, but they never get to be the head on the shoulders. Boss skills are like herpes—you either have it or you don't. And I have it.

The rare times I heard Big Dick's voice was when he whispered in his men's ears, or in that corrupt guard Tony's. Always in a low voice, his hand in front of his mouth. I was impatient for him to confide his secrets in me, to give me missions to accomplish. He'd only spoken to me once—to order me to change the TV channel. I got the shivers, and then it turned into full-on trembling that almost made me drop the remote. I quickly switched to his favourite channel, then started breathing again. Big Dick had an impressive voice: paternal, soft, soothing, like Rick Mercer, the guy that does that funny show on TV.

Television's a big deal in prison—that's one of the first lessons I learned when I got here. I still have the cracked rib to remind me. Most inmates have small televisions in their cells or cellphones for watching their porn or their American series, downloaded before delivery. Yup, even cellphones are keistered in. Hence their exorbitant price, pegged to the size of the screen. As the optimists insist on telling us, this too shall pass.

For sound ambience, there's a television fixed to the wall in a corner of the common area. Who gets to control the TV is like a microcosm of prison hierarchy. Pedo has never chosen the channel. Giuseppe and I try to grab the remote when nobody else is holding it, but as soon as one of the black guys—especially Colossus—rocks up, we hand it over. They in turn defer to Butterfly if Denis isn't there. And whenever Big Dick shows up, everyone shuts their traps and watches CNN. The boss, a shrewd strategist, likes to stay informed. And reinforce his authority. We recognize it immediately in him because he controls the TV and the drugs.

Getting high is a basic need. All over the earth, since the dawn of time, all humans have consumed psychoactive substances. It's well documented. The substances and the methods of consuming them change, but the need for them never goes away. Whether legal or not, prescribed or not, expensive or affordable, we get high with whatever's on hand. Alcohol, GHB, tranquilizers, THC, cocaine, LSD, gas, PCP, ketamine, caffeine, MDMA, nicotine, amphetamines, or antidepressants, the most-prescribed medicine on the planet. You take what you can get. It's simple supply and demand.

Inside, there aren't too many drugs but there are a lot of medicines. Especially in our wing of crazies. We all have diagnoses, more or less legitimate. It's hardly surprising that the pill market thrives in the slammer with all these long-time addicts. If it wasn't that, it would be something else, it's all about availability. Do you really think teenagers would fuck themselves up sniffing gas if they could get their hands on anything better?

The methadone prescribed for getting addicts off heroin is an excellent drug in itself, the one with the highest value within these walls. There's a special way of taking it, since the addict has to drink it in the office, in front of a guard, then regurgitate it back up in their crib to sell it. Hardly any of the people who need it keep it for themselves, it pays too well: nearly a hundred dollars a pop. So you end up with addicts in withdrawal and inmates more smashed than Lady Di's last Mercedes. It certainly makes for an atmosphere. Unfortunately for us, we haven't got any heroin addicts in our wing, so no methadone. Too bad. But dealing in psychiatric medications is still a growth market. Even if they wreck and destroy you, these artificial paradises allow you to survive these very real hells.

And we needed to increase supply. That's what Butterfly told me, handing me a hollow pen. *Have a hit!* Willingly, I bent over and snorted a long line of crushed Seroquel, almost fifty milligrams, I'd say, based on my nose's observations. I sniffed it all up in one go. *Hssshmmmhhaaa!* My nostril was burning, that was a good sign. The drug wouldn't get stuck in my sinuses. I was going into orbit. There's nothing like a hefty dose of anti-psychotics to make you lose touch with reality.

Butterfly liked to make me take something before he forced me to make love to him. It made me more docile. And mostly it made the whole operation less difficult for me as well as getting me a free high. If you can make a bit of profit out of someone exploiting you, at least there's one thing to be said for being submissive.

As he got into his usual position behind me, he told me that from now on I'd be contributing to the medication supply line. I objected that I'd been evaluated at my trial and when I arrived at the prison, and I'd done a whole bunch of questionnaires and psychometric tests. Apparently the results were impressive, but I didn't get prescribed anything. *It would be furpriving if they prefcribed me anything now...* By way of reply, Butterfly contented himself with forcing my head into the pillow to finish off the job.

There was no post-coital pillow talk. He simply reminded me it would be in my own interests to get myself some pills, any kind, as long as they got you high. He couldn't go any higher on his own prescriptions. *If I would just have a bit more...*

If I juft had!

Butterfly was disconcerted, even though he wouldn't have known what the word meant.

What? What did you just say?

It'f not if I would juft have, *it'f if I* juft *had, if doevn't take the condiffional.*

Deep silence. Then, *Do you know where you'll be taking it if you ever try to tell me how to speak again?*

I'm forry, I wav juft trying to help you, if I would juft have known…

He continued, unperturbed, *If I would just have a hundred and fifty more milligrams of Seroquel every day, that would cover my needs. That's the minimum you need to get hold of. You have no choice, this is coming from the top.*

It was an order from Big Dick. There was nothing to discuss. The black guys were getting high more often and had the money to pay for it. We had to provide the merchandise. If the order was coming from Big Dick, that changed things. At long last, here was my chance to shine in front of the boss. *Alright, I'll fort it out.*

It is possible to influence doctors to change test results. We can move around in their probability tables. Just like you can make statistics say anything you want. Here's the proof: statistically speaking, humans have an average of one testicle each. It's basic math.

I was going to have to use my acting talents; I wasn't really mentally ill. Apparently I'm more dangerous than that. I land squarely on Axis 2 of the DSM-5. This means that I, according to psychiatrists and other ignorant medical experts, have a personality disorder. I didn't suffer from any chemical imbalance in the brain, merely from a few irreversible deficiencies in the construction of my identity. On the mechanical side, my head was good, but my personality had been built around cognitive distortions—survival strategies for facing up to the traumas of my childhood. It was all very reassuring.

Personality disorders. That's what the experts at the trial reported. I was impressed when I met them, since I recognized two of the psychiatrists from *True Crime Canada*. They couldn't promise me anything but they said I had a good chance of appearing on the show, that I was an interesting case.

So I asked Edith, the officer monitoring me and my hypothetical rehabilitation, to prepare a request for a medical consultation. *And the fooner the better, pleave.* She said we'd first have to discuss it at our next weekly meeting, which would happen the day after tomorrow. Edith would have to do a preliminary evaluation before sending me to see the doctor. That gave me some time to prepare my argument. If I managed to convince this young guard straight out of school, I'd easily dupe the doctor. You never get a second chance to make a good first depression.

Friday, four o'clock. Professional to a fault, she reminded me about our appointment. As if I might be unavailable, or out, or something. Women need to feel safe. That's why they always choose the strongest men, or the most dangerous. I was very dangerous, and I was single. This led me to start thinking about my only chance of love for the next decade: her.

Edith wasn't my type, and I don't think she was anybody else's either. Brunettes with brown eyes are pretty ordinary. But if you shut a starving vegetarian up in a butcher's for long enough, he'll end up stuffing his face with old dead flesh just like everyone else. Supply and demand once again, as always.

I left her, deep in thought: she would do as a lover while I waited to finish my sentence and meet some real women. After all, if they tolerated Butterfly raping me every day, they could easily accept my having a relationship with Edith. Justice isn't the only one wearing a blindfold.

The idea worked itself out over hours and days, giving me new strength and a spring in my step. The idea of love knitted itself a cocoon where it could transform into an emotion. It worked on my body, somewhere between my guts and my heart, just like magic. The more I thought of her, the less I found her stupid and the more I thought she was beautiful. Love really is stronger than everything. The Beatles, a popular boy band, wrote a lot about that, and you don't get to be multi-billionaires by singing nonsense.

It's unhealthy for men overflowing with libido to stagnate together without any possibility of relieving the tension. The general-population inmates had access to the conjugal visit room and could get spoiled by their wives or mistresses pretending to be their sisters. Or their actual sisters, who knows! But for the inmates under protection, it's a dry regime. Visiting room, masturbation, and assault. It's not surprising if there's a slip now and again.

Since I'd been sentenced, I was less into solitary pleasures. I limited myself to blowing my wad three times a day, since I no longer had access to my zinc cream to soothe my inflamed penis. And the guards doing their rounds, the crushing heat, and having a cellmate didn't really help the masturbatory effort. Even in the shower I was always stressed that Butterfly would come and lean on my shoulder—or lower down. It was settled: a stopgap wife would be good for me. And I'd enjoy stopping Edith's gap.

I was still thinking about my love life as I fed my doves. The hour after the evening meal was the only time we got outside all day, so we had to make the most of it. In our barred cage, under the insults and threats from the regular inmates stationed at the windows of the adjacent buildings, some people walked in circles, others smoked or watched Butterfly lift weights. I wandered to the corner of the enclosure, where my birds were weaving in and out of the fence.

Over the time I'd been feeding them, I'd built a lot of trust up with my mourning doves, a couple of which always flew together. I had to protect their food, some dirty pigeons were always trying to push in. I chased them off with kicks; I never hit them, but it was enough to make them fly away. The doves could then enjoy the bread or rice I'd saved for them. They were comfortable coming closer and closer to me. After three months, some of them would even eat out of my hand. I was like Saint Francis, a famous Catholic Christian ornithologist.

Some inmates mocked me because they were jealous. Even Giuseppe, who would soon be bathing in his own blood. People taunted me, but nobody dared to approach us. A current passed between me and the birds. Something invisible and essential, something indescribable. As soon as they landed in the yard, I couldn't take my eyes off them. I was glued to them. I spoke to them, fed them, treasured them, and got lost in them. Especially when they took off again. They were free to fly over the prison, the city, the world. Unbothered by our borders, our barriers. Then, with pain in my soul, I went back to my cell humming "I'm Like a Bird" by Nelly Cohen.

3

DESTITUTION

It really and truly was a letter from my mother. An indiscreet guard named Paul confirmed it for me. Pretty much. He told me it was personal mail, a long letter written by a woman. It could only be her. Unless Bell has a strategy of harassing former customers even if they're in prison. No, it could only be my repentant mother, trembling with love and lost time. I could already picture myself moving in with her when I got out.

At that time, around mid-June, I still didn't know I'd have to kill again, and so quickly. I was amusing myself with Edith, reeling off a litany of suitable lies and playing at rehabilitation. Polishing my halo cost me nothing, and gave the young lady officer the satisfaction of a nice model inmate.

Guards are human: they like hearing what they want to hear. And that matches up with government policy: nobody ever does all their time. Sentences are meaningless, they just pacify the media and shut the victim's mouths. It costs too much to keep us inside. And people have to dangle carrots in front of us so we don't all kill each other, or at least not too often.

In fact, we only do a fraction of our sentences, but which fraction it is remains to be determined. It's all negotiated in the office of the rehabilitation people with the agents of conditional liberation. You have to give them so much that their files are completely overflowing. From note to note, from therapeutic activity to good behaviour, with a bit of bonus snitching, you end up with an evaluation that means you're allowed back into society. Then reality catches back up with the fiction, and respectable people are scandalized by a rape or murder that could have been avoided. But whoever has drunk, will drink; whoever has killed, will kill; and so on. This is an old whores' tale that I too will honour.

I'm ftill trying, Edith. I'm monitoring the company I keep. I'm working on myfelf. I'm juft one big building fite!

Edith made a note of everything I said, nodding her head vigorously. I guessed she'd give a pretty athletic blow job; her neck could keep a rhythm. She was a young officer, somewhere in her twenties, puffed up with goodwill and hopes of promotion. She truly believed in social reintegration. If she could only imagine everything that went on, all the other types of reintegration, inside the walls of her beloved prison, she'd be quickly disillusioned.

I'm getting ufed to privon life, but I'm ankfiouf about my fycholovhical state, I've had fuifidal thoughtf... I'd like to fee the doctor...to make fure I'm not depreffed. This speech was supported by an incredible acting job, I was really inhabiting the role. I was reaching the heights of interpretation worthy of a young Marlene Dietrich.

She stopped talking, put down her pen, and said, *That's really how you're feeling?* Silence. *You can tell me what you're going through, you really can, what's wrong?* I had tears in my eyes. But I didn't cry. Tears in the eyes is good, as long as they don't fall. I tipped my head back to make sure, took a deep breath, and listed off the symptoms I'd learned about in the prison library. Three cheers for books!

Yef, yef, I fwear, loff of weight and appetite, infomnia, loth of interest, irritability, mood fwingf and even dark thoughtf for over two weekf.

She took a few notes and confirmed she'd send me to the doctor, but in her opinion what I needed most was to be listened to. Silence. The bitch really wanted to see me sob. I thanked her as I raced off to go back to sweat in my cell. I curled up in a ball with my face in my pillow.

Edith attracted and repelled me at the same time. Like a magnet soldered to a spring. Or a grandiose fate plotting its own tragic denouement. Maybe I had the gift of clairvoyance and could already feel, in the vibrations of her aura, the drama that awaited us. *What I really want to know is, as* Lenny Kravitz once sang, his voice full of questions, *is she gonna go my way?*

The emotional tension between us sizzled. I spent more time in her office than any of the other guys she was responsible for, she always called me by my first name and looked me in the eyes, that tells you all you need to know. She didn't turn me on at a genital level but there was something about her that burrowed its way into my brain. And the brain is an extension of the heart.

I admit she'd taken her time winning my heart. I don't want to seem picky, but I should point out that Edith had a pear instead of a body. A willowy head and neck, small shoulders, a slim torso, but an enormous ass. She had the pelvis of a greedy whale. To her misfortune, she didn't have one of those beautiful enormous asses some women know what to do with, firm and rounded at the same time. No, she got to lug around the typical female jogger's bum. Boring!

She was a ordinary brunette, almost cute, who could have aspired to a good-looking partner, but out of the 206 bones in her body, it had to be the pelvis that was the megalomaniac. A huge, wide, fat ass, with no meat to flesh it out. No curves anywhere else either, just width, just ass. It was like one of those graphics showing global wealth: she was very badly distributed.

In her defence, she did have what is commonly called a fuck-me face; she was a sexual woman. There was an unspoken invitation to sex right in her face, from the little lifting of an eyebrow to a smile at the corner of her mouth. And I figured her out better and better as I paid attention to the equivocal signs that she was sending me. Tons of them! Our relationship was heading toward intimacy with the precision of a GPS fresh out of the box.

Friendship between a man and a woman is rarer than a shy reality-TV star. There's always some kind of seduction or desire happening on one side or the other. Whether it's professional, personal, or ambiguous like our relationship, men and women only have sexual relationships. Relationships that might or might not get consummated, depending on the level of beauty, wealth, violence, or charm of the principal actors.

Up to now, I'd basically only fucked ugly women, mainly volunteers. Escorts were often more attractive. But you have to pay for everything, especially prostitutes. I had to face the evidence; I had loved little, and been loved little in return.

I imagined this thing with Edith would be a love as real as it was free. I was determined enough to climb a mountain at the drop of a hat. With a little effort, I could even find her sexy. I wanted her and wanted to fuck her. Wanted to make love to her as well. One doesn't exclude the other, everything in moderation. They play at being all innocent, but women love rough sex, it's very well documented online. There are millions of specialized sites.

Her face was already tangled up in my fate. I used my fox's cunning to keep it close to me: I asked them to give me the prison's administrative manual, *fo I can read about my rightf!* Jocelyn, the unit boss, was suspicious but was obliged to give me a copy.

I spent hours poring over Edith's photo. Among the listings of the guards I hated, she sparkled like a diamond in the sky, reminding me vaguely of an old song. I neglected my reading entirely to concentrate on her photograph, right in the middle of the prison's organigram on page 12. It was like a sex-free porn mag. I was jerking off my heart.

All the guys had visitors in the visiting room. Everyone, and I mean everyone, without exception—except for Pedo and me. The black guys, the crazies, and the murderers all maintained close family ties. Killers' mothers are indulgent, it's well documented. They certainly visit more than the mothers of orphans.

It didn't bother me, I stayed in my cell reading, self-harming or practising my onanism. Obviously I still hoped my mother would come and visit me. Hope is a hopeless burden. Even when it's as thin as a popular teenage girl, it's hard to carry. But life is life and life's a bitch, I sang to myself.

Anyway, right up to the trial my mother persisted in refusing to recognize me. With the dirty fat Greek at her side, she swore under oath that she'd never had a child. I yelled at her to show her stomach to the court, wanting to file her paunch as evidence for the prosecution, wanting her to show off her Caesarean scar. *My* Caesarean scar! In addition, I demanded a maternity test. But it was deemed inappropriate and I was taken out of the room once again.

While I waited for her excuse letter, I brooded on my

bitterness. I felt like a legless tightrope walker as I navigated the fine line between the hope of seeing her and eternal disappointment. It's complicated, grieving for a living person. I can hate her all I want, but I still love her. Like a scab or an itchy wound, I scratch her memory when I feel lonely. I scratch a lot. In prison it's worse, but I've always been solitary against my own wishes. It's not just her fault. I was constantly changing fathers, schools, and social workers. No time to put down roots. I never had the chance. Like the old saying goes, it takes a whole village to neglect a child.

The trial reminded me of it all. Everyone I'd ever known paraded through to kick me down and betray me in the name of justice. Some were angry with me, hurling abuse at me. When I was convicted, I consoled myself with the thought that everything would go back to normal after the judgment. Once the justice system had sentenced me, their resentment would fade and they'd forgive me.

Since I've been rotting away in jail, my only visitor has been my lawyer, who is repugnant and disagreeable. He's also rich and ugly, which makes his presence hard to stomach. Isolation's tough for a humanist. When you feel lonely, the best support often comes from someone even lonelier than you. I consoled myself by going to hang out with Pedo.

Steve Jobs proved that the apple never falls far from the tree. In Pedo's case, the hairy nuts didn't fall far from the palm tree. He suffered from a chronic lack of a model of manhood: he'd had an absentee father as far back as he could remember. His father was already doing time for attacking modesty and assaulting minors, including his own children. Handing it down from father to son: a great statistical reality.

I don't know if the father showed the same level of vulnerability, but Pedo was an excellent whipping boy, which is kinda funny because what else would he want to whip but a boy?

Scapegoat might suit him even better though, with his goat's face and his sullen attitude. Mid-thirties, paunchy, and dirty blond, he had the personality and social skills of a dirty toilet. The one might explain the other.

Pedo might have had a chance to respond to our constant stream of insults if he hadn't been in a permanent overdose. Haggard eyes, pasty mouth, random snickering. More knocked out than medicated. He was the only one who took his medication intravenously, on court orders. This crazy dude was a real psycho.

I heard Louis-Honoré spreading a rumour that our head psycho was also undergoing some kind of chemical castration. If that's true, it's stupid. Pedophiles are sick in the head, not the dick. But whatever, given the way they drugged us up, our Pedo couldn't have been a threat even if he'd been left alone with a bottle of lubricant in a Toys"R"Us.

Scapegoats are absolutely essential when you live in a group. They perform a basic function. First, since they're the scapegoat it means that we're *not* the scapegoat. These martyrs channel the negative energy, and we can console ourselves by comparing ourselves to them. I tried to explain all this to him when I was showing an interest in his situation. But there was nothing there to reconcile me to the human race.

Pedo's real name was Thomas-Olivier Chagnon-Dubé. Whether it was Latin influence or end-of-race consciousness, by saddling him with these double-barrelled names his parents basically guaranteed he'd never have a happy life. And it worked.

I questioned him at length, but I couldn't figure out how he'd ended up in our section. He should have been locked up with the other scum like him, in section G4, the wing reserved for protecting pedophiles, jointly known as the diaper snipers. I guess he was too crazy. But I suspected he was gaming the system, that he had deliberately schemed so he could switch sections. Some debt or threat, most likely. Never trust a chomo:

they're always manipulative and underhanded. Good as the little girl who had a little curl, except they'd rape the little girl.

Life is not like a box of chocolates, it's like poutine. There's rarely one pure, clear taste. Everything's thrown in and mixed up together. You might have more fries or more cheese in any one bite, but everything's swimming in gravy. It's the same thing with life and its problems: alkies are a bit depressed, anorexics self-harm, the schizo dabbles in kiddy-fiddling between two periods of psychosis. People who are obsessed with clinical labelling call it comorbidity. I call it sad reality.

So Thomas-Olivier Pedo-Whatsit was rotting away in our section, definitely not right in the head, probably bipolar and anxious and psychotic and addicted, as well as being a pedophile. They say you can't have everything, but he certainly gave it a good go.

Pedo was serving a long sentence because he'd killed one of his young victims, a distant cousin. He thought he could see the devil in her; he was a classic textbook case of modern psychiatry. He even tasted a little morsel of her. I'll let you guess which part. We talk about how crazies have a screw loose, but this guy had an entire bag of nuts and bolts rattling around upstairs. But he'd been judged fit to stand trial. Whatever, he could barely even paint with his fingers.

I left Pedo in front of the TV and pretended to go back to my cell. Instead I burst into his. As I moved stealthily, my heart fluttered as if the twelve horsemen of the apocalypse were getting ready to ride me. I had to move fast and find some drugs.

I could no longer wait for Butterfly to drug me so he could rape me better. I'd been using too much for too long, I needed a dose right then, just like everyone else in the place. I'd watched my rapist going to and fro from Pedo's cell, and I was pretty sure he wasn't cheating on me. Pedo was too ugly. He had to be a mule, there was no other good explanation for it. He must have drugs, or the pharmaceutical equivalent, stashed away somewhere in his cell.

The seconds were ticking away. I risked capital punishment if I was caught. Stealing is beyond the pale in the kingdom of thieves.

And bingo! A box of Tic-Tacs stuffed in a crevice in the window frame. Time was slipping away. If I was caught red-handed I could say goodbye to my last remaining teeth. I cast a glance around me; the guard was looking the other way. I went back to Pedo, still hypnotized by the screen, even though it was turned off. I turned it on and he smiled.

Denis was always the first one to come back from the visiting room. He'd walk across the communal area and head back to his cell, without even deigning to glance at us. I was burning with desire. He *would* look at me, he *would* recognize me, and sooner rather than later. Denis was going to fall off his high horse and break his neck.

Denis looked like Big Dick but whiter. Slim like his boss, except even skinnier, and a few years younger, in his late forties with an immaculate mane of hair that matched his shirts. He had pale skin and suspicious eyes behind large gold-framed glasses. Just from looking at him, you could tell he was an observer, a visual person with a sharp eye. A day owl. He only ever spoke to Big Dick, but he spied on everything and watched over everyone. On rare occasions he might whisper a word into Butterfly's ear. This was rarely a good sign. Faces would be punched in the next few minutes. But Denis never laid a finger on anyone. He was white collar, he didn't get his hands dirty. He had nothing to prove to himself, still less to other people.

Inside, guys fight, happy for their testicles to take a pounding to show they've got balls. But swelling doesn't make you brave. Denis had internal confidence, the authority of competence. He emanated a quiet strength, just like my librarian, the Sage.

After lengthy negotiations with my lawyer, and backed up by pressure from Edith, who thought the privilege was appropriate for my rehabilitation, management had conceded. I was allowed to leave the protection wing once a week to go to the prison library. Of course, this all had to happen outside the times the so-called normal inmates might use the library, even if the cramped room of the prison's literary pantheon was barely visited. Hydroponics aside, criminals have no interest in culture.

The majority of inmates come from that half of the Quebec population that is proud to be functionally illiterate. They behave by instinct, they're just animals with rights. The intellectuals like me, who know how to read, find this shocking. Democritus, the inventor of democracy, would back me up: illiterate people should have no rights, and especially not the right to vote. They can't even form an opinion from reading the crap the journalists spout.

So I had the four shelves and the hundred or so books all to myself. Or almost. One guard kept an eye on things, and the librarian, the Sage, gave me recommendations.

The Sage was ordinary in every way, so ordinary that he put the common in communism. Around thirty, brown hair, brown eyes, no noticeable features. Not even any tattoos or scars to make himself stand out a bit. A wooden cross on a necklace, but that's pretty standard. God's very popular in prison. Guys cling on to his robe as if they were petticoats. Faith is a pathological manifestation of hope.

You have to jump through a whole bunch of administrative hoops to get access to your mail, your packages, or your lawyer. And it's years before you can hope for a ministerial pardon. God is the last remaining route to instant gratification for members of the penitentiary population whose ability to put in effort has atrophied. And he clears what remains of their conscience. *Truly stupid is he who refuses free absolution.* Epistle of Mark, verse 24, or somewhere round there.

The Sage never smiled. Credit where credit's due. People who never smile are always honest. A smile is just bait, and the biggest fish aren't in the ocean. He was honest but looked stupid. I would soon discover that his notable expression was more down to depression than gangsterism. Which was sad for him; depression kills ten times more people than criminals do, it's well documented.

Being average is dull. I told myself that at least he had a nickname, the Sage. Turned out that Sage was actually his surname, but since I'd been calling him the Sage for months, I just carried on.

The prison library was a pretty small place to contain all the knowledge an uneducated person might need. I'd have burned through the whole lot in a few years, maybe even a few months. Fortunately for me, you could order books. The librarian appreciated my eclectic interests. I got them to deliver everything to us, from engineering manuals to the Hardy Boys, and of course comics. I took up the whole of his little budget. I liked reading everything. With or without pictures, and in my own language as well as the languages of the immigrants, and the thicker the better.

The only genre that left me cold was contemporary poetry.

Whether short or long, it's always boring and wrong. And it doesn't even rhyme! The Sage tried to get me into it. I tried to tell him that my life was already full of poetry, that rap was poetry, but he kept going on about it. *Listen, young man, you can't just rhyme posse and pussy and call it poetry.*

It'f urban poetry, you're juft too old to get it.

And he went on about the wealth of Quebec poetry, and insisted that I read Gérard Godin, Marie Duguay, and Denis Vanier. I like Vanier a lot, he's the exception to the rule. I understand nothing, nada, absolutely not a single word of what he writes, but he does use the words *cunt* and *tattoo* a lot, which is good.

But it was still nothing compared to rap. The proof? Rap sells. I was in a hurry to drop my first album and have those greenbacks rolling in. I had so many ideas for the cover and the title. I'd even polished up some nice Franglais couplets, to represent our culture—or lack of it. The Sage pretended to be unimpressed, but he still asked me to repeat the first verse of my latest creation.

Je suis le best
Cool as fuck
Le hottest rapper in town
Si tu try to fuck
Je te laisse down
Represent Donnacona
From Québec to Canada!
Braaah! Braaah!

Just to annoy me and stoke the embers of our friendship, he swore he couldn't hear a word of poetry in it. He showed more bad faith than a priest. But sadly, it didn't stop me coming back to him. Friendships based on a shared love of books are strange relationships.

Books save lives, especially medical books. And *The Little*

Prince maybe—I guess it could make psychotics feel better about their condition. They might feel less alone and hang themselves less. I'm speculating here. In my case, the library was a refuge, a bubble of shelter away from Butterfly. A chance to get out of my own head. Books are still the best way of escaping, even if you're an inmate in a maximum-security prison. But most of the inmates don't know that. The Sage knew it. He read as much as I did but he remembered more of it. I got the stories muddled up and only remembered the bits I liked or could use. It wasn't about my memory, I'm just more selective.

My librarian admitted he was straight out of Sainte-Madeleine-de-la-Rivière-Madeleine. *It's in the Gaspé.* Obviously that's a long way away; someone must have come from a long line of inbreds to think that would be a good name for a village. When I said that, he almost smiled. *Yeah, maybe. Anyway, I should have stayed there. It was a bad idea to move to the city, especially the suburbs.* He murdered someone in Montreal's northern ring. A crime of passion, like mine. But also a neighbourly crime.

I had to ask him every week, but after a few months he agreed to tell me the whole story. Deep down he was the victim, the victim of those suburban jerks, those little assholes who got laid every Saturday night, those snowblower-lovers.

It was rudeness... Rudeness is the disease of the century, man's downfall. I should have seen it coming, I should have moved to the country and hidden away from the world. The world is grey... Fucking city, fucking suburb... There's always some neighbour who loves crashing his lawnmower into your peace and quiet. At dinnertime... there was always this unemployed Mike Holmes type banging away in his yard...

I listened to him silently, enthralled. I rarely listen without talking at the same time.

It pushed me to the limit… It wasn't the lawnmower on its own, nor the lawnmower and his endless renos. Nor the lawnmower plus the renos plus his garbage can on wheels that he used to park outside my window with its noisy fucking exhaust that always woke my daughters up. It was all that on top of my own tiredness, I think… When I decided to go and talk to him about it, it was already too late, I couldn't find the words. I snatched the hammer out of his hands and then opened up his face with it.

Woah, are you feriouf? You fmaffed hiffkull in with a hammer? I was impressed.

No, his face really… The sinus holes opened up to join his eye sockets… With his jaw pulped, his face was a hole, just a hole full of red mush, and I couldn't stop hitting it. Apparently I went at it for a good ten minutes with his girlfriend trying to pull me off. Even the hammer was in pain… I can't really remember…it was intense.

I'd like to get myfelf a condo one day.

He looked at me for a long time before murmuring to himself, *Yes, it's safer if it's soundproofed.*

4

HONESTY

There were no Tic-Tacs in the Tic-Tac box. This should have been good news. I finally had some drugs, just for me, to take secretly when I was alone like a real druggie, which I always will be, anyway. Despite the withdrawal. Whether I'd underestimated how much I was in withdrawal or whether it was just really good speed, I couldn't say—but it was definitely a big stash.

The theft from Pedo's cell had been discovered. The worst awaited me if I was caught. I prayed to remain an anonymous addict, but nothing was less certain. They'd do anything to get their drugs back, even if it took twelve steps.

That evening the tension was so thick it would have taken a chainsaw to cut it. Denis was going from one cell to another, talking to Colossus. Butterfly was fuming, banging his fists on the table and looking round at everyone. I was afraid he would literally rip my face off before the end of the evening. I absolutely had to get rid of my loot before they started searching. I raced into my cell and gulped down the five orange pills. I'd already ground up a couple and snorted them an hour earlier but couldn't feel any effect. The five remaining pills I swallowed down, with difficulty, with a big glass of nothing.

Once I was rid of the fruits of my crime, my relief was short-lived. The pills themselves could no longer incriminate me, but I had a corpse on my hands: the box. I thought about swallowing that too, but that seemed unrealistic. Other orifices crossed my mind, but it would end up coming out one way or another. I had to think of something, and fast.

Too late. Butterfly and Denis appeared in front of me. The twin towers crashing down on a New York junkie. I was going to die.

It has to be him, the fucker, he was alone in the wing with the other crazy. Denis didn't take his eyes off me.

I held the Tic-Tac box in my right fist. I would have let them cut off my hand rather than be caught with it.

Did you find a stash of pills, you ratfucker? Butterfly started the interrogation, Denis chimed in, and I panicked.

I-I haven't done anything. I haven't taken your pillv, Bu-but-terfly.

He was gripping my chin when Paul, the guard on duty, showed up in the doorway. *We're done here, gentlemen. Be so kind as to let go of each other and leave the cell until quiet time. We want the whole lot of you where we can see you.*

It's hard to admit for a gangster like me, but a correctional officer saved my life that night. Or at least bought me some time to find a way out. Closely followed, I went to sit next to Pedo, who was still high as a kite. While my accusers were sitting down opposite me, I placed the incriminating box on the crazy man's lap and then put my hands back on the table. All I had to do now was weather the storm and stick to my story.

I never went in Pedo'v fell! The guard would have feen me, you can afk him. I wav alone watching TV and Pedo was in hiv fell. Maybe it wav him that hid your pillv.

The inmates at the adjacent tables were hanging on to

every word of my defence. *He's so bullshitting you, Butterfly, don't believe a word of it.*

Denis whispered in his henchman's ear, keeping his inquisitor's eye trained on me. I could hear the questions he was asking, but Butterfly reworded them and added a few swear words. Everything went silent whenever a guard went past. The session was dragging on, I could tell they were going to go from sentence to execution in the same breath. Would it be a classic stabbing? Or the more sporty option of jumping on my head with both feet together? Or would they go down the erotic route and just get Butterfly to poke my eye out the next time he raped me?

After this had been going on for a while, Paul called Pedo over. It was time for his evening injection. I kept my hands well in sight on the table at the moment when, after being called two or three times, Pedo finally stood up. Click clack! The Tic-Tac box tumbled to his feet. *Fucksake, it was Pedo having himself a little party all along…* Philippe put the evidence into words. I turned white, Butterfly was pale, and Denis smoothed his hair back with an incredulous smile.

Never again! The word of someone hooked on multiple drugs is as worthless as that of a drunk, but I believed it. No more unknown pills for me. I survived a long night of paranoia. As if the stress of the interrogation had just been a warm-up, I didn't sleep a wink the entire night. Really. I didn't even manage to blink. All my nerves and muscles were in a state of extreme tension. I couldn't move, talk, or jerk off, and I spent the night just hoping to make it through to the morning. My heart was being dribbled at forty beats a second by an epileptic god. Crazy pills. They're a powerful stimulant; I see why the guys were so keen to get their hands on them.

The section's criminals showed better judgment than most judges and recognized Pedo's lack of responsibility. He wouldn't be punished, they'd find another cache in his cell, and prison life would continue as before. Breakfast was relaxed, almost bucolic. We just needed a few bunches of dried flowers to complete the scene. Compared with the tension of the previous day, our section was finally loosening up and chilling out. As was I, luckily, since I was going to have to give another incredible performance. Playing a mentally ill person takes focus.

The doctor looked like a quack: he was tired and had a moustache. He was as professional as anything, which made me suspicious. He asked how he could help me. Procure me your finest psychiatric drugs, my good sir, so I can impress this goon and climb up the criminal hierarchy of my wing of the prison... I didn't put it quite like that. Instead I listed off the symptoms I'd learned off by heart, with my defeated expression to back me up.

My heart was pounding in my chest. BAM! BAM! I was afraid of breaking a rib from the inside. I gave it everything I had, abandoning myself body and soul to the performance, more determined than a pole dancer in debt. I was aware that I had everything to play for, sitting on that little plastic chair, with Dr. Moustache in front of me and Jocelyn, the unfriendliest of all the guards, behind me.

The notorious Jocelyn, the boss of the cell block himself. The only one among them who was fair, straight, and consistent. What's the point of giving us a guard who can't be manipulated? He might as well be a robot. I hoped he wasn't going to intervene during my evaluation.

If I couldn't manage to get myself a prescription, Butterfly would beat me up and rape me more brutally than ever. Worst of all, I'd lose my chance to impress Big Dick. I had to give it everything. I emphasized each symptom, explaining that it was becoming more frequent and increasing in intensity. I bit my cheeks until they bled to give me a good expression of unbearable pain.

The doctor casually stroked his moustache. *Mmm-hmmm…*

I thought: *Mmm-hmmm what, for fuck's sake? Are you going to give me my smarties or not?* The doctor ran his index finger along his jaw and looked at me with a face that veered between suspicion and compassion. I had to convince him right away. I had to turn myself into a woman and start in with the trembling and crying. Go!

I thought of my mother, my mother who screams, my mother who loves me, my mother who kills herself, my mother in the ambulance, ripped from my love by social services. My emotional-neglect trigger had kinda atrophied. Dry-eyed and panicking, I thought next about finding my mother again, that same bitch who came to testify against me at the trial. But the tears still wouldn't come; all I could do was clench my fists, my eyes filled with rage more than sadness. Then a picture of Edith came into my mind and shot straight to my heart. Edith a few days earlier, worried about how I was doing. Edith of the soft voice, saying I needed someone to listen to me.

Dr. Moustache handed me the box of tissues. I wiped away my tears, proud and disturbed at the same time. *I don't know what to do anymore, waah, privon, waaaah, it'f too hard, I want to die.* I had it in the bag. Butterfly would get his drugs and Big Dick would be sure to give me more important missions. But the doctor wanted one final confirmation. Holding out the last tissues, he stood up, looking over my shoulder. He spoke to the unit boss, asking him what he thought of my mental state, and if it had deteriorated.

I turned to look at Jocelyn, my gaze more imploring than

a depressed spaniel's. He seemed surprised at being spoken to; he came out of his daze and the suspense seemed to drag on forever. *Well, I couldn't really say, he's not my case, you'd have to ask Edith. All I know is that he sees a lot of violence, all kinds of violence, every day. If it was me, I know I'd be deeply depressed.*

Thank you, Jocelyn! I swung back to face the doctor and waited for his verdict. I was like a kid in a candy store, wanting to know what kind of pills I'd get.

As I was being escorted back to my cell, I thought of Edith again, and about the physical reaction I'd had when I thought of her before. I'd achieved my goal of fake crying. But I'd seriously had difficulty with the stopping part.

You're not that bad, you know, not a lost cause, anyway. Jocelyn was beating the same drum again. What did he know about criminality? Just because he swims in it every day doesn't mean he knows how deep it flows. Looking at the countryside doesn't make you a landscaper. But I played along.

No, I'm not bad, juft human. As long as nobody's looking for me.

On the percentile charts for murder, I'd put myself at about 82 per cent. Just like with gayness, there's a spectrum, a ladder, with each rung having its own name for a murderer: accidental, impulsive, passionate, sexual, professional, and—the most glorious of all—serial killer. I aspired to be professional, and maybe even a serial killer. Sadly, the two are incompatible, since organized crime doesn't appreciate its assassins drawing attention to themselves.

You're still young. What do you plan on doing when you get out?

Actually, I plan on becoming the boss of your section while I'm still inside. Then big Mafia boss or serial killer. *I don't know, maybe get my welding lifenfe?*

He liked that. *Good idea. The world always needs welders.*

Does it, my ass. All the factories are closing down one after another. I might as well become a telegraph operator or work in a bookstore!

On the threshold of my cell, just to humiliate me in front of Philippe, Jocelyn carried on being friendly to me. He even put his hand on my shoulder, the jerk. As if it wasn't bad enough being seen talking to a guard, now he was touching me! *I saw your humanity back there. That's a big deal. You've given me fresh hope for you.*

I wriggled away from his grasp, hoping my fellow inmates had missed our tender little scene. *That'f right. Thankf.*

I took shelter in my cell, in my bed, in my head, in a book. To give myself something more pleasant to think about, I took inspiration from the genuine article: Oscar Wilde. He was a real role model, a tough guy. He wasn't a wimp or a queer.

Butterfly was proud of my success. *I knew he'd give you something strong!*

I beamed, happy to have carried out my soldierly duty. I'd brought some decent swag back: strong antidepressants, tranquilizers for daytime, sleeping pills at night, and some herpes cream. That was less useful for my homies, but who knows, it might come in handy one day. I took advantage of this to subtly press my case for promotion. *Fee, I can do tonv of thinv for you guyv.*

He was only listening to me with half an ear. *Thinv?*

I swallowed and tried to articulate. *Thingf, I can do thingf for the organivation. You fould tell Big Dick that he can truft me.*

He smiled at me, but I had to stop arguing my case just

then. It's hard to talk with your mouth full.

To the great joy of my jaw muscles, Philippe interrupted us. Normally Butterfly would have thrown him right back out of his own cell, but there was a warden with him. Fellatius interruptus for poor Butterfly. He told me to meet him by the showers after lunch. I agreed in a manly way and got up immediately.

My roommate was rummaging through his wardrobe and grumbling. Paul had told him that if Philippe couldn't find the completed authorization form, Paul wouldn't give him his package. In solidarity, I took the opportunity to demand my mother's letter. *If you don't give it to me, I'll report you!*

It was still going through the approval process, they repeated to me once again. It's the kind of bureaucratic long-windedness that only prisoners and Franz Kafka can understand. Philippe came out on top this time though. The paper in question, duly signed, was all crumpled up at the bottom of his overstuffed drawer. The warden handed him his opened package, meticulously pre-searched by the prison officials.

I eyeballed his haul as he emptied the box. Cookies, letters, aftershave, and—hidden in three tubes of toothpaste—pens! Lots of pens! I took advantage of this to get him thinking about my tattoo project again. No, I didn't have any money and no, I didn't want to negotiate with Colossus. I argued that since I was his cellie he should cut me a deal, or we could swap a tattoo for a favour or service. You have to understand that tattooing is the poor person's plastic surgery.

Alright, I'll carve you something simple, not your samurai or any of that nonsense. Just an outline tat, but you have to wash your feet three times a day—deal? Taken aback, I had to confirm what he was asking for. *Waffh my feet three timev a day?*

They seriously stink to high heaven, man. It's like you're dragging dead skunks around. It's worse than rotting meat. I'll finish off your awful Chinese character tattoo on your neck, I'll put flames or something around it, but you're gonna wash your feet morning, noon, and night. Take it or leave it.

When I was a kid, my mother used to tell me my feet smelled. But after that I didn't have anyone to tell me. Philippe was bringing back some strange memories. When you don't have many memories, even the bad ones seem good.

The needle pierced the skin on my neck. It burned, but I had to stay focused. We had to talk pretty loudly to hide the machine's noise, and stay alert enough to stop everything and stash our tools if a guard came to the cell. I wondered who, in the end, surveyed each other more—warden or inmate?

Philippe and I hadn't really talked much before, so I took the chance to get to know him a bit. Maybe I'd recruit him into my gang when I'd climbed the ladder. After six years in prison, he still maintained his innocence. On his lawyer's advice, he'd pleaded psychosis in court but got screwed. And ruined. *I've never been screwed like that before, man, never. Like the most expensive whore ever. But she's gonna pay for it too. Let me tell you, man, just because someone screws you doesn't mean you have to come!* The lawyer's plan bombed. Not only did Philippe not get a reduced sentence, but he also ended up in the crazy wing like me. I didn't call him out on that last point.

We shouldn't have gone anywhere near his court experiences. I already believed him, but he kept repeating over and over that he was innocent, that he was the victim of a miscarriage of justice. I felt him getting more and more aggressive, and the machine's needle sinking deeper into my flesh, even while he was swearing to me that he would never have killed his wife, that he didn't want that, that he still loved her. *But that lawyer, man, that lawyer. If I ever get out of here…*

I tried to make him laugh, to relax him a bit so he didn't slit my throat with his needle. *Lol, Philippe, everyone'v innofent here.*

But no, he was really innocent. He maintained that he'd only been criminalized since being inside. He used to have a quiet life with the wife he loved, whom he'd never once hurt, *well, except that one time at the cottage…but I would never have killed her!*

Before prison he'd never been beaten up, never dealt, never taken any drugs. A long sentence really deflowers innocent people. With a single bad judgment, he'd gone from neat portrait painter to tattoo artist in a max-security prison. And he wasn't a very gentle tattooist at that. I could feel blood trickling down my collarbone.

But that picture was worth a thousand swear words. Philippe the Filipino had painted beautiful blue flames around the Chinese character on my neck. A neck that was all red and painful for the moment. It hurt, but I didn't show it. You should never show your emotions in the slammer, unless it's anger, aggression, hatred, rage, bitterness, resentment, disgust, revulsion, exasperation, disobedience, dislike, or irritation. That was pretty easy for me, I'm hard as nails, even if I do listen to Édith Piaf in secret. We all have our Achilles heels.

Inmates actually hide less in their assholes than they do in their hearts. We don't express our emotions but we have them well under control. It's amazing, but hardly anyone commits suicide in prison, in proportion to our ongoing distress. It happens more among the general public, but if you put the general public in prison, there'd be a massacre. We make pretend attempts from time to time, like sending up a distress flare, or to get a trip to the hospital for a change of scenery. But we really don't kill ourselves all that much.

I could have kissed him! If he wasn't a guard who'd dedicated his life to controlling mine, I'd have taken him in my arms and squeezed as hard as Charles Atlas. The great Paul had gone via the office to bring my mail. I was sweating with gratitude, trembling, struggling to open the envelope. At last I had my mother's letter in my hands.

It wasn't a letter from my mother. It was actually from Denise. Some unimportant woman who'd loved me once upon a time. She was bald but kind, and she'd taken care of me when I was a child and my mother was busy committing suicide and getting better. She said she was sad for me. She'd followed my trial in the news. She'd thought about it for a long time before deciding to write to me, but she felt she had to. She said that she knew me, and she knew that deep down I was a good person, that I'd been a wonderful kid. I could get in touch with her if I wanted. But I wanted my mother. I wanted to die. I wanted my mother.

I'd find my mother again before I died.

I threw the letter away without letting it get me down. It was all driving me up the wall, so I took my anger out by punching the nearest wall.

The next day was Saint-Jean Baptiste. All the inmates would celebrate Quebec's triumph on the Plains of Abraham. Ha, just kidding. We were just going to get drunk with Gilbert's hooch. The only times we discussed politics, it was just a pretext to provoke the immigrants. Just like Jacques Parizeau said the night of that rigged referendum, *If we have lost our country, it's because of all that ethnic money and those stolen votes!* That always sets the scene for a good debate.

We were allowed a second helping of dessert, blue Jell-O, and a special evening activity. It was never anything special, but the inmates' committee lobbied the prison to put on some entertainment four or five times a year. *Let them have bread, Jell-O, and circuses!* All they needed to ensure social peace was to let us feast our eyes and our mouths, and our bellies.

That year, to celebrate our beloved country that will never exist, they coughed up some cash to bring us a storyteller. We're not talking Stuart McLean obviously. He'd have cost an arm and a leg, and they'd probably have been afraid of us taking him hostage. He was all about the coast-to-coast Canadianness. But the guy who showed up was just a plain old storyteller: unknown, paunchy, and full of goodwill. It was a long evening for him.

He was already in rough shape when he arrived in our section. He didn't stand a chance. He was ending his tour and his evening with us. The guys in the other sections had already ground him down. We were watching the TV news when he turned up. The bottles of rotgut had been going around for a few hours too long. Everyone in the section was wrecked. Except for Big Dick, Pedo, and me. Big Dick hadn't touched a drop. Sadly for me, my turn was often skipped, and it didn't come round all that often in the first place. And Pedo was permanently on a different planet, so nobody had even thought of offering him a swig.

Our Sunday storyteller must have been practising all week. He put on an earnest performance of "Little Red Riding Hood and the Seven Dwarves," as if he hadn't told it six times already in the other wings. Only his tense features and his distressed face betrayed him. To be fair, he did manage to make the guards—the many guards—laugh. It was an unusual evening: swigging hooch was more or less tolerated, but we had four guards watching us.

Edith was there, my very own Edith; I didn't take my eyes off her. Or barely. Only to give Tony the evil eye. Tony the bastard corrupt guard, who wasn't doing his job properly since he was too busy holding Edith close and whispering sweet nothings in her ear. I took note of his lecherous ogling, his nonchalant predator look, just like shopping-mall sleazebags the world over. Tony wanted my betrothed. There was no longer any shadow of a doubt under the sun of my hatred.

Good old Tony, the man of the moment, pumped up on protein shakes, wearing his groomed little beard styled to look like scruffy regrowth. It was just a shitty neat-and-tidy style designed to show off his handsome square jaw. And my beloved was laughing at his pathetic little chit-chat!

And at that precise moment I realized I loved Edith, because I wanted to slaughter Tony. Jealousy is the only real proof of love, this is well documented.

Even when you're expecting it, violence takes you by surprise. While I was fantasizing about what I was going to do to Edith—and what I was going to do to Tony—the storyteller yelled in fright. Two good hollers. *Aaaaaaaahhhaaaaah!* And it was nothing to do with his tale of "Little Red Riding Hood and the Seven Dwarves." Timoune had jumped up on a table and was ripping Giuseppe's face to shreds. His beautiful white teeth were shattering under the deluge of blows. In the time it took the guards to call for reinforcements and get out their pepper spray, all the prisoners were on their feet circling round the fight, encouraging the Haitian to kick the Italian's head in. International relations at their best. All round the room, the black guys were nervously watching the little crowd, afraid that a third crook would jump in to the fray or take advantage of the chaos to stab one of them.

It was a great fight under the rules—prison rules—treacherous and savage. All the inmates were enjoying the drama; usually we hardly ever got to see any action inside. Blood, dull thuds of punches, shouts. Bam crash, pfff! Timoune was paying homage to his voodoo ancestors, who were thirsty for some blood.

Before the agents managed to separate them, Timoune started trying to rip off Giuseppe's face. Whistles, a harsh alarm, and tear gas signalled the end of the round. We were forced to get down onto the ground while they got control of the situation and handcuffed the attacker. Two agents managed to haul up Giuseppe, who was still conscious, thanks to all the adrenaline. He fainted in the corridor. But before he went through the door, in the reflection of the sentry-box mirror, he threw us a look that was full of vengeful promises. His red eye, shot with humiliated Italian blood, was screaming *I'll be back!*—just like Rocky in *Terminator 2*.

It took four of them to carry Timoune out, one warden per limb. Louis-Honoré celebrated in Creole while Jocelyn ordered him to shut his mouth in Québécois. He'd be doing at least two weeks in the hole. Real hard time. Once the hero of the hour had been taken out of the section, things calmed down. The guys were laughing, already reminiscing about Timoune's battle feats, exaggerating a detail here and playing one down there.

When they announced we were all going to be confined to quarters for the next twenty-four hours, we heard someone sobbing. All the guys, lying on their stomachs, turned to look in shock at the communal area. Pressed up against the garbage can underneath the wall-mounted television, trembling like a pansy in the wind, our great storyteller was weeping big fat tears. That got his last laugh of the evening out of us. We were cheering the sobbing man so enthusiastically that Jocelyn had to bang on the table with his nightstick and threaten us with a second day of being locked up.

Our Sunday Saltimbanco would always remember his trip to prison. He'd never forget that the best intentions can never triumph over the worst individuals. His age-old tale of "Red

Riding Hood and the Seven Dwarves" was granny's home-baked tart facing off against a slice of reality pie.

In the school of life, truth doesn't come from books.

5

AMBITION

The national holiday wound up with a flagpole-polishing session, every man for himself. A whole day in our cells. For those like me with no money to buy a cellphone or to save anything for personal consumption, all we had left was dreaming or self-love. Masturbation is less vigorous in prison. You stretch everything out for as long as you can. Even for a bunch of killers, killing time isn't easy.

At least it gave me a break from Butterfly. It was welcome—it gave me a chance for a bit of self-care. But I had to ration my own amusement since I didn't have any zinc cream. I changed hands, soaped them up, or practised tantrism. Tantrism is transcendent. Getting turned on without touching yourself is the equivalent of cooking for other people—you need to be a chef to appreciate it. I'm the Gordon Ramsay of the hands-free wank. I kept my erection up for more than an hour just by thinking about Edith over and over again.

The morning was dragging on. I was daydreaming about my career, coming up with ways to get into the highest levels of organized crime. First of all, here in prison, and then, once I got out, in the country. And why not go international? My English is pretty good. Nothing is impossible, but if you dream small you'll stay small. On the other hand, you have to match the action to your dreams. Dreaming just for the sake of dreaming is like jerking off and then crossing your fingers for a baby.

I had to make a name for myself, get on TV. I could ice all the inmates in my section, with a bunch of guards as a bonus, and go down in history. Or escape and kill a ton of people on the outside. People would take me seriously. My face would be on a loop on every channel, my name would be on the radio, and all the journalists would be constantly promoting me. I got drunk on these glorious dreams and compared myself to the greatest criminals of all time.

All geniuses, misunderstood by definition, have to go through a period of being held against their will at some point in their career. Al Capone, Nelson Mandela, and Amy Whitehouse are excellent examples. This downtime was temporary: I'd soon find a way out of my position as underling and start shining in the galaxy with the big guys. You just have to believe it, believe in yourself. From serial killer to gang superstar, success depends less on strength or courage than on ego. You have to be able to think abstractly about everything and everyone so there's only yourself left, and this self must be more important than the entire planet. That's the key, better not lose it.

Why did Colossus have Giuseppe beaten up? I jumped, yanked out of my reverie. Hours had gone by without Philippe saying a word to me, since he too was occupied with jerking off.

No idea, maybe fome debt? I stood up and sat down on the edge of the bed. Philippe did likewise.

He wouldn't have beaten him up like that just over a C-note.
I dunno…but how do you know how muff it wav? I was

curious, but above all jealous. How could Philippe, a peon of my own caste, be in the know about the outstanding debts for our section's gang?

Maybe he owed them more, but I know that the Italian guy owed them at least that, for a tattoo I did for him back in April, a dragon on his shoulder.

I mumbled in agreement and let him carry on talking.

I guess they thought he was taking too long to cough up the payola. Now we were getting to the part that interested me.

I'd like you to advanſe me a tattoo av well. If I was going to be stuck in a cell with a tattoo artist I might as well get some ink.

Man, are you stupid or what? You've just seen a guy get his face totally smashed in for a debt and now you wanna get into debt?

It wouldn't be getting into debt, it would be investing. Tattoos get you recognition in my field. And that was without taking into account that I was sure to get a little something, via Butterfly, for the new supply line I'd opened up for Big Dick. And even if I didn't get anything, Butterfly wouldn't let the black guys smash my head in. I had to swallow the pills in front of the wardens, in the office, and then spit them back out in my cell. If I got sent to the nurse or the hospital, every dose I took on the outside would be a net loss for the organization.

And if worse came to worst and Colossus turned against me, it would set off a gang war from which I would emerge unscathed. It was all good, I had a plan in place. I hadn't stolen two-thirds of *The Art of War* for nothing.

I'm ſeriouſ, Philippe. I want you to do my ſamurai tattoo on my back.

Forget your samurai, man, you haven't got the money to pay for it. I'm not wasting ink for nothing. The nice thing about closed doors is that they open the doors to lying.

Nobody elſe knowv yet, but I've ſtarted working for Big Dick… I'm going to have the caſſ to pay you.

His surprise gave way to his sense of duty. *It's Colossus you need to pay, and then he gives me my share. Keep that in mind, Colossus is the one you're going to owe. Three hundred big fat ones for a tattoo like that... You don't have anyone outside who can pay for you, you never have any visitors. If I give you a tattoo, the minute they unlock the cell doors you'll be walking out with a fucking big debt. Are you sure?* Philippe gave himself some serious airs for a Chicano designer. He should read *The Secret*, then he'd see that nothing happens for no reason. And the opposite too. *Hundo P! Get your maffine ready.*

The rest of our period of confinement was taken up with him creating a masterpiece on my back. In spite of the pain of the needle jabbing at me, I sat proud and silent, more focused than a bushido. I visualized every stab as a pearl being inlaid into my back, as a gem that would give me special powers, like a shower of diamonds falling on my body.

Beauty is not being afraid of being ugly. That's a lovely quote from Mick Jagger, who was a sex symbol from the last millennium. Every hole the needle pierced in my flesh was one step closer to glory and power. I was becoming good-looking. Philippe's machine buzzed away for hours, reverberating around our cell, and interrupted only by meals and medication, which both of us had to spit back up for our superiors' benefit.

Philippe and me, we got close. Having someone touch your back for twelve hours is bonding. We talked of everything and of nothing, but less of everything. I reckon we solidified a great friendship. He even gave me some cookies his sister had sent him.

My mother didn't cook, but I didn't eat much. Maybe the one explains the other. I'd have liked someone to send me cookies too. Chocolate chip or macadamia nut or peanut or almond, even though I hate almonds. If my mama sent me cookies, I wouldn't share them with anyone.

After the period of confinement, we still had to wait another ten hours before we were finally allowed to go out for a breath of fresh air. Fresh is a relative term, since two major highways passed close by the prison and a nearby chicken processing plant filled our lungs with its toxic vapours. But it was still good to get outside.

In one corner of the wire enclosure, Denis was talking to Colossus. From the faces they were both making, it looked more like a disagreement than a friendly chat. Denis was pointing his finger threateningly at Colossus's face. Timoune's outburst in our section must have got Big Dick really pissed. Maybe Colossus had forgotten to warn him in advance. Or maybe his foot soldier had acted on impulse. Or maybe, to my great astonishment, it was just that the big boss had wanted to hear the end of the fairy tale and felt cheated.

I stayed in my corner, happily feeding my mourning doves. There were three of them, my usual couple and one other, a smaller bird. I bent down to the ground to let the big male come and peck straight from my hand for the very first time. I was overjoyed, my projects were all coming together, it was a sign. Nostradamus himself could have confirmed it for me, but he's dead.

But when I got up—surprise! Louis-Honoré's face was four inches away from mine, taking into account the height difference. I'm lean, thin, and muscular. He's a stocky, beefy little guy, like Mike Tyson in his good years. I was afraid he wanted to whisper a secret in my ear so he could rip a piece off it at the same time. *I hear you show real initiative, kid, I hear. Seems like you took advantage of the lockdown to get yourself inked, right?*

Yeah, I got a nice—

Shut your trap, fucker, shut your trap. You owe us five hundred bucks for your shitty samurai, got it?

It wav three hundred, Philippe faid three hundred! Things were heating up. All the guys were turning to look at us, and the guards too. Louis-Honoré whispered a few last threats before heading back over to Colossus.

I had a week to get the money deposited into their account on the outside. If not, the little massage session they'd given Giuseppe would be nothing compared to what I'd get. Louis-Honoré was pretty creative when he told me what he was planning to do with the pieces of my body. Big Dick and Denis hadn't missed any of it. Which was good, I was going to need them. It was time to checkmate the chequebook.

I didn't let fear take hold of me. In spite of all the space my terror took up, I still saved a bit of room for courage. I didn't regret anything, no, absolutely nothing; my tattoo would open more doors for me than it would close, even if I had to kill to crack them open. I just needed to stop shaking, stay brave, and be patient. Rome wasn't burned in a day.

You seem more stressed than usual, is something wrong? Edith, Edith, Edith, how can I seduce you, manipulate you, and reassure you all at the same time? *No, it'f fine, nothing feriouf. I'm juft having fome weird thoughtf, that'f all...*

She was wearing her eternal grey uniform, far from the colourful underwear my imagination had been dressing her in these last however many nights. But I noticed she'd unbuttoned the top of her coarse grey shirt, which revealed part of her bosom: sending a big message there!

You know you can confide in me, right? I'm here to keep you company through the hardship of being in prison. I have power over you and have to monitor you, but I'm also supposed to support you.

You can tell me what's on your mind, what's worrying you.

You'll fall asleep in my arms so you can wake up in my heart. No, that was too intense. *Happiness cares about no man, but I care about you.* Too weak. *You're a fallen angel.* Worse still. I decided to be evasive and mysterious. Women love that. *I think everyone needf fomeone, even people who have no one...*

Edith held my gaze for a long time, a really long time. There was a chemistry fizzing between us that you could have cut with a knife. Eventually her plump lips broke the silence. *You know you can trust me, right?* Here we go.

I can truft you?

She nodded her head softly, sensually. There was nothing but the two of us, no more prison, no more uniform, no desk between us. She said it again, leaning on each of the words. *You can trust me.*

It was better than an *I love you.*

Yes, Edith, you can truft me too...

6

DETERMINATION

Blood flowed along my thighs before disappearing into the drain. But I wasn't a young girl celebrating her first period. Although I think I'd have liked that. Life is easier for women, girls especially. Less violence to submit to or dole out. Pyjama parties, pillow fights, hot chocolate. Nicely put together outfits. And more tenderness, more affection. I'm not a man who needs much of that kind of thing—my heart's pretty stony. But all the same, I'm pretty sure that behind every psychopath is a little girl just hoping for someone to stroke her hair.

The scabs and encrusted blood washed away under the hot water. In the mirrors over the washbasins, opposite the showers, I managed to twist my neck to see my new tattoo. It's tricky, seeing your own back; the way my skin twisted kinda wrecked the way the work looked. What I could see, and what I liked, was that the tattoo covered almost my whole back. It was impressive. I was burning with the desire to see it up close. I'd need to ask a guy with a cellphone to take a picture.

This fake good idea soon passed. The only such person I was on relatively good terms with was Butterfly. I wouldn't have dared ask him, for fear he'd try to take some erotic photos. I didn't have any choice about being his fuck buddy, sure, for however long it took me to climb up the hierarchy, but I couldn't allow any proof of it to remain. It might come back to bite me when I found myself at the top of the crime pyramid. Or the political one. There's a revolving door between the two.

I was going to get out of the shower, followed by Pedo, who was snickering away at nothing, when Denis came in. His mere presence set all the nerves in my body jangling. I was going to press myself up against the wall to let him pass when the prophecy finally came true. Denis, notorious and respected criminal, Big Dick's right-hand man, spoke to me. Me! There was contempt in his voice, but he was still talking to me! *Go to the boss's cell at twelve twenty-five on the dot.* And that was it: the dice had been thrown in destiny's face.

My rubbery legs barely carried me to my cell. I had to look good for Big Dick. I only had twenty minutes. The boss was going to entrust me with an important mission, or announce that he'd settled my debt with Colossus, or kill me. No, he wouldn't get his hands dirty, Butterfly had already had a gazillion chances to strangle me from behind. It could only be good news. I was champing at the bit.

I suffocated myself when I cleaned my teeth because I was singing at the same time. *Danfing queen, danfing queen, I am the danfing queen!* I couldn't keep control of my body. Philippe noticed, and asked me what I was so excited about. I told him I had a meeting with the big boss of our section.

Well yeah, you did say you worked for him.

Okay, so maybe I got a bit ahead of myself there. But now it was really happening. Sometimes, if you lie with enough conviction you can fool everyone, even reality.

My trembling feet managed to get me out of my cell, which was the one nearest the guard's room. I had to walk across the whole communal area to get to Big Dick's cell at the far end. The meals were being delivered. In prison, we don't just eat shit figuratively speaking, we get three square meals of it every day. Like animals, we have to take what we're given. Anyway, nothing can be remotely appealing when it's served on a beige tray.

Colossus and his brute sat down to dinner next to Gilbert the moonshiner. They weren't talking to him, but he wasn't bothered by it. He was happy just to make his hooch and do his time in peace. It was hard to believe he'd chopped up a tenant who hadn't paid his rent. But, after all, even the sweetest chihuahua is descended from a wolf. We should never lose sight of that.

Louis-Honoré watched me as I tried to put one foot in front of the other. *Five hundred dollars, you fucker! We'd kill you for less than that! Maybe we'd even do it just for fun.*

I passed Philippe and Pedo, absorbed in some crude program with a summer theme. Scarlett Johansson was being beamed in. Philippe was testing the limits of his jail buddy's deviancy. *Come on, Pedo. Have you seen this chick? Check out her face, her thighs, she smells like sex up to here, man. You can't tell me this doesn't turn you on more than a little boy.* Pedo just smirked and stared at the screen.

At the moment I approached them, Denis came out of Big Dick's cell and stood in front of the door frame, as he did for each of the boss's meetings.

I noticed that only Butterfly was missing, and then realized that Tony was the only one working on the floor, and that the office door was shut. Butterfly was having a follow-up meeting with his officer, Fat Mireille. With Timoune in the hole, the count was good: I'd be alone with Big Dick. Just four more steps and I'd be there. One. Two. Three.

And then Denis stood in front of me, blocking my way

to the inner sanctum. *Everything you're going to hear and say in this cell stays in the cell. Look at me when I'm talking to you! Am I making myself clear?* He didn't need to be so forceful, I'd fully grasped the seriousness of the situation.

Yef, I underftand, it'f the omertà. I really like the movie. I'll never know if he watched it too; he just shook his head and swore.

Under the curious, and even envious, gazes of all the guys in the section, I went into Big Dick's office. It was a bit of a disappointment. I don't know what I was expecting, but his crib wasn't luxurious in the slightest. The *Extreme Makeover* team would have had their work cut out for them. In fact, his cell was just like mine. But with no decoration, no graffiti, no grime. Not even a postcard of a bikini-clad whore, nothing. And nothing lying around either, no dirty clothes, no special-interest magazines. Just pure minimalist feng shui. Just Big Dick, sitting on the edge of his bed. That was enough.

The boss was whispering into his cellphone and scribbling in a black leatherette notebook. It was a big phone, a BlackBerry, I think. Respect to the person who smuggled that in. Big Dick waved at me to wait a minute. I'd been hoping for this meeting forever, a real genuine boss who wanted to talk to me, I would wait as long as he wanted me to... *Yes, that's right, twenty G... I'll call you back. Do what you have to do.* He hung up and indicated I should sit down on the opposite bed, Butterfly's bed!

He was making me nervous. I tried to put things into perspective: there wasn't much to be impressed about, he wasn't the chief boss of all the bosses in Quebec, just the boss of our wing, and the crazy wing at that. But I'm a sensitive guy, so I stammered a bit.

I-I'm here, Bi-big Dick, I-like you wanted.

With a wave of his hand, he ordered me to come closer. Near him. I slid along the bed until I was facing him. My knees were almost touching his. I'd never been so close to a big man. He cleared his throat. *You can call me Gilles.*

P-pardon? My mouth was drier than the Sahara during drought season.

My name's Gilles. You can call me Gilles.

I was terrified. *Okay, Dzilles.* It seemed dangerous to me that a man of his moral fibre would want to become intimate with me so soon. Had Butterfly recommended my services? Was this sudden closeness part of a sex game whose rules I didn't know?

I need you, kiddo, I need you and you need me. You have guts. Getting yourself tattooed by Philippe without going through Colossus sure takes guts. And I saw you getting excited when Giuseppe was getting his head kicked in. Do you like violence? Are you the real thing?

The right answer, quick. *Yef, Mifter Dzilles, I'm the real thing!*

He leaned toward me and put his hand on my shoulder like a father. And I don't mean the kind of father who abandoned his son to unbearable suffering without ever trying to reach out to him again.

If I had a delicate mission, a very delicate mission, do you think I could count on you?

I could hear the glorious violins, the chords of *The March of the Emperor*, resounding with the imaginary drums. Pum pum parrrrrrrum pum pum.

Are you going to give me an answer or what?

Oh yef, Mifter Dzilles, I'll do anything!

He leaned forward and stared right at me with his fathomless eyes.

Even stab Butterfly?

Time stood still. It pressed down on me with all its weight.

There had to be a right answer. And this right answer had to come from my very own mouth. But I didn't know what it was. Was this a test of my loyalty? Was I being offered a new job— going from service fuckhole to paid assassin? Lives were at stake. Mine, without question, and maybe Butterfly's too. It was too stressful. I wanted to run away and pee, preferably in that order. I no longer wanted to be there, I wanted to be anywhere else, even in the hole with Timoune. Too late. Denis was blocking the way out. Big Dick was holding me by the shoulder, and I had to play: all or nothing. He who has nothing risks nothing. *Yef, I could even kill Butterfly.*

Denis nodded his head at Big Dick, who let go of my shoulder and congratulated me. It wasn't a test, he really wanted me to eliminate his right-hand man.

You're the best man for the job, he won't suspect you, you have an...intimate...relationship, and you're brave!

I was trembling with pride. *Yef, Dzilles, yef, I've got real ballv in my heart.* I couldn't get over it, the big boss was giving me a murder contract, what a promotion!

But why him?

Big Dick insinuated that the order had come from outside, that the Italians were proposing some staff changes, but Denis interrupted him. *Stop, Gilles, he doesn't need to know this!*

Big Dick agreed, which blew me away. He took orders from Denis? Was this gang organized crime or a communist co-op? If it wasn't the latter, there was some confusion over roles. Big Dick pulled me out of my thoughts by confirming that I would kill Butterfly with a knife.

But I haven't got a knife! He waved his hand to show that this was a minor detail. *Let me speak, we've got no time to lose. We'll get you a knife. You're going to kill Butterfly when you're alone in the showers or in your cell, on a Tuesday or Friday night, that part's important. It needs to be a day when the guards are doing office stuff. It has to be just Tony on the floor, do you understand?* I nodded, not daring to speak. *Stab him in the neck or the chest, whichever you want, but you have to do it properly, you need to be sure you kill him, okay?*

I hadn't stopped nodding my head since my last answer, so I just carried on.

Kill him and get out of there. You need to leave as soon as you're sure he's dead. Tony's in on it. We're going to set Timoune up to take the fall. I wasn't nodding any more at all. *But Timoune's in the hole!* Big Dick smiled. *He's getting out today, it's all set up.* This was a big plot with a lot of complicated details. I tried to understand all the angles. *But won't Coloffuf—*

Never mind Colossus, let us handle the politics. Just focus on Butterfly, that's plenty for you to worry about. Prepare yourself psychologically, we'll get you your weapon by the end of the week. If you do it properly, you'll start working for me officially. And we'll have something big for you, something really big. He signalled the end of our meeting by answering his phone, which was vibrating non-stop in his pocket.

When I left the boss's office, all eyes turned toward me. The other inmates couldn't believe that Big Dick had had a private chat with me. If they'd known why, their jaws would have hit the floor. I carried my own newly recruited jaw with pride. All the attention was on me, the rising star, until Denis barked: *Nobody saw anything, this meeting never happened!* As everyone went back to what they were doing, Tony came out of the shower area and got back on "surveillance."

With my gait more confident than ever, I went back to my cell. You couldn't hear anything except the ineffective fans, the noise of my footsteps, and the washed-up TV host clinging on to his summer show. He finished his indulgent interview with Scarlett Johansson. Philippe was still needling Pedo. *Look at that thigh, Pedo, look at that muscle. Just think of the pussy rodeo you'd have if she climbed on top of you!* Pedo had stopped snickering, his haggard eyes lit up suddenly and he mumbled, *No, Hayley Mills in* The Parent Trap...

When I went back to Louis-Honoré, he seemed to feel obliged to go over the numbers again, but without any insults this time. *This doesn't change anything, you still owe us five C-notes and you're gonna pay!* Without bothering to answer him, I continued on my way just like Alexander the Great Napoleon. I got back to my cell at last, threw myself on my bed, buried my face into the pillow, and yelled with joy as I forcefully humped the mattress. *Fuck yeah!*

My joy was short lived. The guard who had come back for the cart with the trays had given the alert and sounded the alarm. His colleagues came running, and the section was filling up with guards. We were ordered to stand outside our cells. Right now! A butter knife was missing. *Hey, we'd butter find it fast! Hahaha!* The agents didn't like my joke, nor did my fellow inmates. *Hahaha*, I pretended to laugh for a bit longer to hide my unease.

If the knife wasn't returned in the next minute, we'd be entitled to a full-on shakedown. *We'll turn over every single cell, and body search every inch of your guts if we have to!* Jocelyn yelled. He was the kind of guy who really liked his lunch break. Having to organize an internal purge because of a premeditated murder was totally not a valid reason to deprive him of it.

This was a big deal. They even cut short Butterfly's meeting. Butterfly came out just before I, his would-be assassin, did. Nothing would ever be the same again. He was dragging his feet and grumbling. The fear he inspired in me, the pains in my ass and in my soul, hatred, resentment—all that was making way for impatience. My enthusiastic impatience about stabbing him to death.

Butterfly got back to his cell and stood in front of it. Philippe came to stand next to me. *What's going on?* With my mysterious silence and knowing looks, I showed him that I was in the loop about what was going on. Big Dick and Denis came out of their cell last. As soon as they set foot outside, Colossus burst out at Big Dick, *You're gonna have some explaining to do!*

The wardens pulled on their latex gloves while Jocelyn, his watch in his hand, announced the countdown. We'd earned ourselves the works: a minute search of the cells and a full body search for each of us. *Using cutlery is a privilege, not a right! We can take it away from you, and that's exactly what we'll do if nobody has returned that knife in the next forty-five seconds…thirty… twelve… You asked for it!*

What should have happened didn't happen. The knife was conspicuous by its absence, all the cells had been searched. They'd found loads of stockpiled medicine, a few precious amphetamines, Gilbert's brand-new batch of hooch, and Philippe's tattooing machine, a more significant loss. But we saved the essentials, the big-ticket items: mobile phones and the famous knife that hadn't shown up for roll call. A weapon inside a prison is worth more than the American Constitution to a Texas redneck. Priceless.

Just the body searches left. Luckily, I saw Fat Mireille heading over to look after me. I'd have preferred having Edith service me, but at least it wouldn't be a man fiddling with me in public. Fat Mireille made the most of this rare chance to touch young flesh. She palpated me vigorously from my heels to the top of my head. The only thing she could have found was my enormous pride at being part of Big Dick's gang. But she didn't discover anything.

I noticed that Tony was searching Denis—Denis, who never sweated, who never talked to Tony. And I noticed a droplet trickling down his temple. And I saw his lips moving. And I knew then that he was my weapons guy. No doubt he'd given the corrupt agent an order. Tony immediately finished and announced that his body search was over. Often the best way of seeing things is to not see anything at all.

Each of the agents involved in the searches affirmed the same thing one by one. Jocelyn was fuming, convinced that something big was being planned in his section. A metal knife, even a butter knife, could become a fearsome weapon in the hands of a skilled craftsman. There'd already been one murder and two attempts in the prison since the beginning of the year, he didn't want one in his section. *We're not going to drop this— everybody in confinement!*

Colossus clenched his teeth and his fists, angry at having been relieved of his personal stash of medicine and the tattoo machine. Gilbert was congratulating himself on having distributed his rotgut the previous week. Big Dick and Denis were staying stoic. Pedo was still snivelling, wanting to go back into his cell. And Butterfly was yawning like an idiot, completely oblivious to the fact that all this commotion was directly related to him. As for me, I was rejoicing.

They'd gone to a lot of trouble to get hold of a weapon for me. I'd been promoted at the speed of light. I would no longer just be an impulse killer, an almost accidental murderer, and with extenuating circumstances on top of that. I was becoming a hit man, with all the notoriety that comes with it. The best movies and the coolest video games are based on a hit man. Or two. Or a whole bunch if it's Tarantino.

Hit man or no hit man, I was still going to be confined to my cell. Jocelyn was promising us some bad conditions, he was prepared to go as far as he could within the legal limits. And for as long as the knife remained missing, our meals would be served with plastic cutlery.

Before we went back into our cells to hole up, all of us inmates observed, assessed, and suspected each other. Who had the knife? Why? Denis and I exchanged a quick, complicit wink, but he didn't look at me. Along with everyone else, I took one last lungful of air before going inside. *Clang!* All the doors were locked at once, with a heavy metallic ringing sound, controlled from the sentry box.

Now, though, they were no longer locking up a beast in a cage, but a free man, a man free to reach his destiny.

7

LOVE

I dreamed about Edith. I read in *Reader's Digest* or some such scientific journal that hearing other people's dreams is basically one of the most boring experiences for a human being. But that won't stop me from telling you about mine.

The scene was taking place in my childhood bedroom, the one I had between four and four and a half. We moved a lot. Edith was lying naked on my bed—a mattress right on the floor—wearing just a red garter belt and torn silk panties. She was aiming a pump-action shotgun at her waxed genitals and screaming, *My pussy, my pussy, don't kill my pussy!* I tried to reassure her, to shout that I loved her, but my mouth was full of butter knives that slashed my tongue every time I attempted to speak. This went on for hours, this impossibility of communicating that was as good as any contemporary autofiction. I shouted and she threatened her pussy. Then I yelled and she aimed the gun closer. Eventually she shot herself in the vagina bellowing, *Everything is possible!* And then I woke up. I wondered if a psychologist would find anything worth analyzing in it.

Philippe kept me company for the rest of the night. My scream of terror had alarmed him. I'd have taken the chance to get another tattoo, but his tool had been confiscated. I was willing to bet that Jocelyn had no intention of giving it back.

I don't know who nicked the knife, but he'll have to settle accounts with Colossus. Usually I get a warning when there's going to be a shakedown, and I have time to take my machine apart and get it all hidden away. My tongue was itching to taste the secret. After all, I could allow myself a little indiscretion, he was my roommate, my tattoo artist, and even kind of my friend: he'd given me cookies.

I think the flight of the butterfly will be scythed down by the wind... I sat back to enjoy the effect.

What? Are you writing poetry?

No, I hate poetry! It'f more of an allegory, I wav anfering your queftion.

Hey? What question? Philippe rubbed his eyes, sleep and lack of culture stopping him from figuring out what I was saying.

You were wondering what wav going on, who ftole the knife. I wav juft giving you a clue, that'f all. And I stretched out on my back, hands behind my head, with just the right amount of emphasis in my sigh.

You're going to kill Butterfly? My sidekick jumped up and leaned over me, well and truly awake now, more excited than Pedo at a public swimming pool. *You! You're going to kill Butterfly?*

That'f not what I faid, but you can believe what you like.

Disbelievingly, he said, *Yeah, right.*

I squashed his doubts when I revealed that I'd been promised a place in Big Dick's organization. Now he wasn't looking at me the same way anymore. He sat down, rattled. This guy, who'd witnessed this brute being so violent toward me, who had to sleep in a cell that stank of sex, who thought I could never get things turned around, he now realized that he'd underestimated a potential killer. He'd judged me all wrong.

Our closed minds are prisons where truth gets away from us.

Man…I'm freaking out… You? Come on, man… Philippe was trying to take the information in. He lay back on his bunk and tried to search out the meaning of life in the concrete ceiling.

He didn't have to look that far. Tell me who you hate and I'll tell you who you'll kill. In my case, it all fitted together. Butterfly. If affection is the desire to stab someone in the face, then I had a lot of affection for him.

Getting rid of him. It was all I could think about, apart from Edith, and my mother, and Big Dick, and freedom. But mainly about crushing the insect under my blade. I knew I was capable of assassinating and I was keen to set to work. It's the first murder that gets stuck in your conscience, after that it gets easier. I had a spiritual vocation for it, a calling for bumping people off. I would kill again, it was decreed. Once a tiger has tasted gazelle flesh, he doesn't want to eat grass anymore, it's too late. He becomes a natural-born killer. I was that wild beast on the rampage, pacing in his cage, full of rage. Did you pick up on my awesome rhymes there, by the way?

Through the small rectangular grille of our window, dawn was turning the sky purple. A new day was rising, along with my reign. I practised a few ninja moves in the middle of the cell. *Cha! Kyakai! Takata! Hmmph!* My voice was more confident, my body moved with the grace of a Siamese cat. I trained for hours under Philippe's perplexed gaze. I went right to the end of the night, right to the end of my strength, until Edith came to take me out of the cell.

She was beautiful that day, more beautiful with every day that passed. She had her hair down, which was unusual and a pretty big signal. She asked me again, personally, how I was doing. A woman in love is an open book, open at the heart page. I could read inside her. She was torn—she didn't know how to pursue our relationship without wrecking her career aspirations. She was becoming attached, and I was going to tie the knot.

I truft you, Edith, but it'f hard for me. My mother wav taken away from me when I wav very young by agentf of the ftate, like you…and my father used to beat me.

She was touched, opened her mouth a little and let out a compassionate little oh.

Fometimef he tied me up and forfed me to crawl acroff the floor to my plate, which he put nekft to hiv bulldog'f bowl. If I wanted to eat I had to prive my tiny porfion out of hiv mouth. And devvert wav alwayf a thraffing.

Jackpot! She was touched, her eyes were wet. All upset about my father's mistreatment of me. Ha! If only she'd known that the reality was far worse: I'd never even known my father.

She picked up a tissue, blew her nose, and pulled herself together. She couldn't let her emotions get any more hold on her, her mascara was too cheap. She changed the subject. *You need to understand that some things can stay between us, even if it could have a big effect on stuff in this prison. We said we could trust each other.* I noticed that she was wearing pink nail varnish on her short nails. The flirt. The naughty little flirt.

Yef, I like knowing that you truft me, Edith.

I want to tell you that if there are things that you might say or admit to me here, I would never use them against you, quite the opposite. She wanted me to make the first move, to make our connection official. I could already picture the scene: when she found out that I wanted her too, she'd stand up, go over and lock the office door, and in the same movement take her clothes off slowly while she danced for me. I wondered if she'd have a waxed pussy like she did in the dream.

I think there'v fomething fpeffal you want me to admit, babe. I flashed all my teeth at her in a smile, or at least all the ones I had left.

Where's the knife? Straight in there for the shot. Like a eunuch, it was impossible to see it coming. Her plan must be to use me first as an informant before taking me as a lover. Nice strategy, I liked it.

The guard in the box saw you going into Big Dick's cell with Denis. You've never had much to do with those guys before. Did you steal the knife for them?

Whoa, Colonel Mustard, I didn't take the knife, I didn't kill anyone in the living room. I have no idea what you're talking about. I decided to play the game, hardball. I dug my heels in, crossed my arms, and my legs, and everything else, to underline my inflexibility. If she wanted foreplay straight from the pages of a crime novel, I'd give it to her. *You're barking up the wrong tree, I'm not a fnitch, babe.*

First off, you're not in a situation where you can call a guard "babe." Second, I just want to help you, keep you out of trouble. I know deep down you're not a bad boy.

Women, hey? There's nothing like a nice mix of bad boy and intellectual—like me—to get their hearts thumping right down to their G-strings.

You're not a bad boy, you're just impulsive. You have a gift for finding trouble. It's like you plow right into it. Those guys aren't exactly choirboys, they can be really dangerous. I nodded.

Why were you in Big Dick's cell when his bodyguard wasn't there?

She wasn't playing. I felt dizzy, breathless, all the clichés. Her voice had trembled on the last words, her gaze was full of worry. She was afraid something bad would happen to me. I could have kissed her.

I'm going to give you the intel, but it's juft becauve it'f you and we have a relationfip. I'm not a fnitch, I hate rats.

Her face lit up so much it was practically fluorescent. *Yes, I*

understand, *but you're right, we have a relationship based on trust,*
you can tell me anything.

She reminded me of those high school chicks, those
unattainable nymphettes who used to write wise sayings in the
margins of their agendas: "Love without trust is like a flower
without perfume." I was going to give her a little spritz of perfume. If she wanted to have her cake and eat it, and get the butter
knife with a cherry on top, that's what she would have. Without
compromising myself, I was going to give her just enough hints
so she could seem in the know around her superiors.

I can tell you that the butterfly iv going to go back to being a
poor little caterpillar. I let a silence fall so she could read between
the lines.

But she read faster than I was expecting. *You're going to kill*
Butterfly for Big Dick? Fuckety fuck, she was like the lovechild
of Agatha Christie and Columbo.

No, no, that'f not what I faid! I didn't fay that at all. I'm not
gonna kill anyone!

She was leaning toward me, intrigued, her enormous ass
barely perched on the edge of her chair. *Why would you go into*
the boss's cell then, were you taking him the knife to kill Butterfly?
You clearly have something to do with it.

I hated myself. I should have known that any woman interested in me would have to be intelligent, astute, and perceptive.
I had to get myself out of this tough spot fast but protect myself
at the same time. *Timoune'f going to do it! It'f got nothing to do*
with me, they juft wanted to warn me that Coloffuf iv going to try
and pin it on me.

She sank back in her chair, confused. It made her look like
a sexy secretary, I'd have to get her to wear glasses sometime.

Big Dick wants to protect you and he's also planning to assas-
sinate his henchman?

She was pretty smart at summing things up. I hoped she'd

be happy with this version and it wouldn't come back to bite me. If not, like usual and like Bill Clinton, I'd just deny everything.

That might be true. We knew some kind of attack was in the works, something involving Big Dick's gang and Colossus's. The order must be coming from outside...

She had more information than I realized. Obviously when they're locked up and under full-time observation, the guards have the time to construct various theories about their prisoners. And to soil their souls by turning them into informers. *Yeah, but I think that if the black guyf manave to kill Butterfly, it will change the balanfe of power. Fo I need to make fure I don't get caught in the trap, fo that Timoune'f the one who copf it for hiv own crime and fo I replafe Butterfly...*

She looked as surprised as if she'd hiccupped. *So you replace Butterfly?*

I couldn't work out what was so surprising, apart from my slightly clumsy indiscretion. In all the excitement of scheming, I'd let her see my cards. *I dunno, I wav juft faying that for no reavon, but it'f not relevant. Let it go.*

I had to shut my mouth, change the subject. I'd stuffed it full of lies to hide the plot. But lies are like soda crackers: they're dry. You have to wash them down with a bit of truth soup. And right now she was getting too much truth. Imagine what she could fish with all the bait she was worming out of me.

I needed a diversion, quick. *I'd really like uf to fee each other more often, babe.*

She smiled, tensed, and hit the ball back. *Yes, that could be useful for both of us. You're a very interesting prisoner. But I have to remind you that we aren't in a place where you're allowed to call a correctional officer "babe."*

She wanted me to keep the terms of endearment for more intimate moments. The time for clasping each other on her desk had arrived, I could feel it right in the marrow of my bones. But

83

there was a knock at the door.

Edith stood up, swayed before my very eyes, slowly, so I didn't miss any of her swinging hips, then opened the heavy door. Jocelyn again, that great, tiresome man with his brotherly urges. They had a whispered conversation in the doorway. The unit manager didn't take his eyes off me. His eyes were brown, like mine, but they didn't have the mischief or intelligence that mine have. He thanked Edith before indicating that I should follow him. As I passed her, my girlfriend gave me a sweet promise: *We'll talk again soon.* That was enough for me to leave with a full heart and full of desire.

From the office that adjoined the sentry box, it was just a few steps to my cell. Just enough time for Jocelyn to let his mask fall and threaten me.

Listen up, don't take me for a sucker. Edith trusts you. I'd like to trust you too, but something smells off. You're mixed up in something. I've got my eye on you.

I didn't give a shit about him keeping his big brown eye on me. His eyes weren't even as shiny as mine. I had Edith on my side, Edith, who found me very interesting. And the most powerful gang in the section to protect me. That jerk was mistaking me for a run-of-the-mill crazy. Well, mister, I'm a se-ri-al-ki-ller!

I don't know what you're talking about. I'm not mikfed up in anything.

He slid shut the heavy door of my cell to return me to confinement.

Poor old Timoune, barely out of the hole and already suspected of planning an assassination. But the guilty ones never get burdened with the burden of proof, especially in a prison setting. You can scream blue murder all you like; you have little chance of hearing the echo of justice.

Edith was cleverer than Jocelyn, but she trusted me. And that made me the cleverest one of all. With the corrupt Tony on our side, Edith would come round to directing her attention at Timoune rather than at me. In the end, my indiscretions would help Big Dick's plan. He'd realize that as well as being an unparalleled serial killer, his new soldier had a sparkling mind at the unarmed end of his arm. Edith had almost got me to say too much, but I'd got myself out of it without any damage. From now on I'd need to avoid the subject. In less than twelve hours I'd told two people about Butterfly's imminent death, and one of them was a correctional officer. Denis and Big Dick might have some concerns about my methods.

Filipinos can be nosy. Philippe's questions flowed freely, he tried to confuse me, wanting to know who was going to do what, what Big Dick's plans were, how I'd managed to seduce Edith. He couldn't get over the fact that she'd pulled me out of my cell so we could fuck on the desk. Obviously I hadn't actually quite reached that stage, but close enough. And Philippe stayed amazed: in two days I'd gone from insignificant roommate to Mafioso Don Juan.

I was kind of doing more than the customer was asking for, but I have an image to uphold. And he couldn't check the truth of what I was saying; like a lesbian at a girls' sleepover, I had it pretty easy. And it was all moving so fast. It wasn't long until the murder, and love was already aflame.

Edith filled my mind and my body with every breath. It could only be a shared love, there was too much for me alone. An emotion that big can only be felt by two people. *Take your partners*, as they say in pole dancing.

I was embellishing a little further with each conversation; Philippe, an excellent audience, was asking for more. I told him all about my fantasies until they finally let us out of the cell after another thorough and pointless search.

They found nothing so they had to let us get back into the normal routine. There was a committee of prisoners that monitored prison conditions and made sure they didn't become too inhumane. Good idea. We all met in the common area the second the cell doors were opened. You could have cut the tension with a knife. The famous missing knife, in fact.

Colossus headed straight for Big Dick, but Denis intercepted him; it was weird to see two men fighting in whispers. From what I could make out, Colossus didn't like cutlery disappearing when he hadn't been warned about it. On the other side, Denis had to remind him of Giuseppe's attack and the section hierarchy. Watching them shake their index fingers and murmur so forcefully, you'd think you were witnessing a diplomatic incident.

And Pedo went off to crash in front of the TV.

And Gilbert started leafing through the last three days' papers.

And Louis-Honoré reminded me that time was passing by holding up four fingers to indicate the four days that had gone by. He then smoothly changed those four fingers into two—a revolver pointing at me. A pretty creative little move.

And Butterfly grabbed my arm and guided me to the showers. In spite of its being the end of June, with the air heavy and the humidex through the roof, I would gladly have skipped the hygiene routine.

The guards usually respected the prison custom of turning a

blind eye to inmates' sex lives. We were rarely disturbed when we were playing with ourselves or having love made to us by force. I never figured out if it was down to Edith's jealousy or the guards' vigilance, but Butterfly wasn't permitted to relieve his tension that day. Still in "prevention" mode, they'd put a third guard on our floor, Dany, who followed us to the showers and watched us like a hawk. To my great joy, that thwarted my undesirable lover's inspiration.

He still ordered me to get undressed and wash myself. He'd take care of me later; he wanted his sex toy to be as clean as a whistle. I was resignedly getting undressed when I heard Dany laugh—Dany, that pathetic asshole of an insignificant guard— which made me freeze in position. Butterfly figured out what had made him laugh just before he asked me to turn around, and then he burst into idiotic laughter too.

Those two hilarious jerks thought my big beautiful five-hundred-dollar tattoo was basically the funniest thing they'd seen in the last decade. And it set them off again, seeing my samurai brandishing his katana either as some Chinese guy grasping his erection, or as an alien wearing a cassock and waving a pool noodle about. I turned away, but Butterfly refused to give me my shirt back and threatened to smash out my other teeth if I didn't turn around again.

He was cackling and calling the other inmates to come and have a cheap laugh at me when Jocelyn intervened to bring back order. I felt a hint of gratitude toward him, but it was barely perceptible amid the hatred and resentment pulsing through my veins. Butterfly wouldn't be waiting long for my revenge; he deserved his imminent death.

I took my irritation out on Philippe, ordering him to meet me in our cell, where I give him a serious roasting. I made sure I shouted loud enough for all the other inmates to hear me and realize that I was superior to him from now on.

Do you think I'm an idiot? You've given me a terrible tattoo! It doevn't even look like a famurai!

Philippe defended himself: he was a portrait painter; he'd never drawn a samurai in his life, his specialty was faces and lettering.

Good at fafev, my aff! It lookf like a Fineve guy. Famuraiv are Japaneve, not fucking Fineve!

He tried to calm me down, assuring me that Butterfly and the warden were exaggerating, that it wasn't that bad.

Don't give me that! The end of the weapon'v round! I wanted a katana, a thin ford, not a fucking gladiator ford! It'f like he'v holding a big phalluf!

Philippe didn't know what a phallus was. I had to splutter in his face and explain to him with multiple images. He tried to negotiate: he'd rework it as soon as he got another machine, he could improve it.

Mother Tereva iv leff dead than my faith in you! Eat fit and die, you've done enough damave!

Red with rage, I left him alone in the cell and went to zone out in front of the TV. All the guys were laughing, except for Denis and Big Dick, who were smiling.

The gangs were closing ranks at either end of the common area. The future of our section was being plotted in little cliques. It was weird—rather than gathering in their cells to have their little chats, the two gangs were posseing up in the common area. They were making their presence felt. Taking ownership of the territory and showing that fear was unknown to them.

The professionals on high saw this as a return to normal. In any case, they had to take their third guard off the floor. The budget came first. Two days of extra staff is all the state can provide to keep the officers and pariahs in their charge safe. If you're bold enough to stick your head in the wolf's mouth, pull it out quickly before the jaws snap shut. The guards were on edge.

We'd gone back to our coercive sexual activities, our habits, and our small-time dealing. Giuseppe wouldn't be coming back, his lawyer had managed to get him transferred to a lower-security prison—one that would be more secure for him. A lot of good it would do him. Denis lost his roommate and ended up with a loft all to himself.

As the token intellectual, I could finally leave the morgue-like atmosphere of our wing to go and renew my library books. In the library, the Sage wanted the news from our section. *Tongues are wagging all over the prison. Apparently something's brewing in your neck of the woods. I mean, three days in confinement. What's going on?*

I can't talk to you about it, but fomething iv going on and I'm going to get a promofion.

The Sage, the man with the most depressed face in the entire prison, lit up. *Noooo. Are you planning an attack? An escape? You're not going to kill someone?*

I'm not in a pofifion to confirm that informafion. A supporting wink put him on the right track. His face settled back into its condemned-man look.

Too bad, you're amusing, I like seeing you come by.

I reassured him immediately. *Don't worry, I'll be back. I have a plan...*

The Sage raised an eyebrow and then suggested I read Machiavelli's *The Prince*. I didn't want to read a knight story, so I borrowed some tales about mutants by Isaac Asimov.

🐦🐦

Two days had passed without movement of troops or shift in mood. We endured the heat wave as best we could, letting our disgusting food get cold—even grosser now that we had to eat it with plastic cutlery. Some people took up to five cold showers a day, or made themselves makeshift fans with pages from the newspaper.

Luckily, the criminal milieu gave up cowhide a long time ago. Now leather is the prerogative of gay guys with moustaches and fetishes. And retired people. Now we wear tracksuits, which are more comfortable. Especially when we have to train between two men addicted to protein powder. "We" excluding the person writing: I don't need muscles, I can handle firearms. I improve my talent with visualization: having a gift isn't a given.

By lunch we were sweating like pigs when Butterfly surprised us by attacking Pedo. He got up from the table, headed over toward the mindless idiot, grabbed him by the collar, and dragged him for twenty feet. Right to the box, where he flattened him against the window and called him a snitch. We all got up and went after them, yelling at Butterfly to give us a good show. *Kill the fucker, kill him!* We needed some kind of action, we're only human. *Come on, Butterfly, you can do it!*

All the guys were crowding around them. The guards were trying to disperse us when I felt a hand in my underwear. By the time I'd grabbed the wrist attached to it, I recognized the caress of a cold blade on my sweaty scrotum. I was blinded by fear; I froze. But Denis reassured me, pressed against my back, murmuring in my ear, under the shouts of the other inmates: *It's gonna happen tomorrow.* He let go of the knife, pulled out his hand, and let Jocelyn get control of him. I stepped back too, pretending to be afraid of getting pepper-sprayed. But we didn't care about that. Only the smell of urine bothered us.

Pedo was sent to get cleaned up and Butterfly was sent to

the hole for twenty-four hours. He hadn't hit him, after all, just threatened him a bit. Threatened for no reason, on his boss's orders. His boss who wanted to create a diversion. A diversion to give me the weapon. The weapon for killing him. Him, Butterfly, my rapist, whom I was going to kill and then replace. Everything fitted together. It was beautiful, well played, I could see the artistry in it. Sometimes you find refinement where you least expect it.

With the background agitation of the guards, I went back to my cell. I heard Jocelyn complaining that they couldn't keep us confined, but they weren't allowed to have more officers on duty either. He'd had an assfull, in spite of his heterosexuality. The summer was hot, too hot for his liking. He verbalized his discomfort with a stream of cursing, while everyone, minus Butterfly, went back to their places. Colossus was more confused than ever.

It was a magnificent dagger. It was indeed the missing butter knife but sharpened on a cement block or homemade file. It was pointed and sharp. The handle was covered with a face cloth tied up with a shoelace. To avoid leaving fingerprints, but especially for getting a good grip. You can injure yourself when you're injuring someone, it's well documented. You need to get up some momentum, especially if you want to kill them. All it takes is a broken rib or cartilage for your hand to slip, and then the whole thing backfires, spraying blood all over you.

The future was about to arrive; my life was going to be transformed. Like Lotelance the day before getting knighted, I recharged my batteries, isolating myself in my cell so I could spend time reflecting. I had peace, Philippe no longer dared to approach me. I focused on visualizing the following day's events.

A meeting between me, Butterfly, and Timoune in the showers had been set up. I'd be lying in wait, a Bengal tiger crossed with a cheetah, ready to pounce when my prey was distracted. Big slashes of the knife to the neck, the chest, the eyes: finally I would have revenge on Butterfly. Timoune and Tony, as spattered with blood as me, would leave the scene immediately, leaving the weapon and the brute's corpse behind them. The only thing left to do would be to give our witness statements. Two against one: *Timoune did it!* And Edith would wrap everything in her good faith, trusting in the confidences she'd heard in a professional capacity.

I went over the plan in my head, again and again and again, trying to sniff out the flaw. What if Timoune wasn't there? What if Butterfly defended himself? What if Tony told the truth? There were so many variables I had no control over. I had to have faith in Big Dick as well as in my destiny. I stayed sitting on my bed for hours, meditating and caressing the blade in my underwear. It was a solemn, sacred time, maybe even spiritual.

I took advantage of Philippe's not being there to caress myself. The excitement of the impending mission bubbled up in a sexual urge. Eroticism and violence are never far apart, which is how we get brutal sex and domestic violence. Eros has been taking Thanatos up the ass with a studded strap-on since the dawn of time. It's well documented in the Lascaux caves.

I slept like a baby that night: I woke up at two a.m. whimpering. Big events are hard.

8

STRENGTH

The big day had arrived. And it was my birthday as well. Twenty-two, Christ's age. Apparently he died when he was older than that, but he must have done something impressive at twenty-two as well. Old Jesus was pretty prolific.

The sun was shining pointlessly behind a ceiling of grey cloud. Finally a bit of coolness, a respite from the heat, a change! The signs were piling up like the fifty-two cards in a Tarot deck. And if all that didn't bode well for my first contract, Fat Mireille showed up to take me to a surprise meeting with my love.

Fat Mireille was a woman in the broadest sense. Massively obese, borderline morbidly so. She could have worn an asteroid belt. And no refined finishing touches. I wouldn't have been surprised to see her scratching her balls and growing a beard. There was no doubt about it: she was equally ugly everywhere. You could guess at her varicose flesh under her coarse grey uniform. I followed her irritated and mumbling body with a smile. The more I thought about Mireille, the more beautiful Edith seemed to me. The grass is always greener when you're inside.

Edith had tied her hair back, another sign. She wanted me to take her seriously, to know that she and I were solid. A surprise meeting between two follow-up appointments, that's not nothing. Girls—especially women—are sly. Once they pass twenty and are old, there's no spontaneity left in them, only calculating and seducing. I could see her game. She was talking to me about my time in prison so she could get some information in her files and look all professional, but all she really wanted was to spend more time with me. I fascinated her.

We aren't allowed CCTV, we don't have enough staff to monitor you all properly; we need you! Silence. I *need you!*

I cleared my throat. *I need you av well, Edith.*

She recoiled in her chair, unsettled. She tried to take back control by changing the subject. *It's impossible that Butterfly would attack Thomas-Olivier without any reason, it was all just a diversion, I'm sure of it. Tell me what's going on in this wing, we can stop something bad happening.*

My beautiful love was all excited, hyped up at the thought of talking crime with a real criminal, a genuine tough guy. She was actually trembling when I told her there were rumours going around about riots and about how major accounts would be settled in the chaos. Edith was sniffing after promotion like a pig hunting out truffles, she was wriggling on her chair. *Tell me what, tell me who!*

I told her enough so she could shine at the team meeting, now it was her turn to give me something. *If I had to leave thif privon, if I wav tranffered fomewhere elfe, would we fee eacf other again, Edith?*

Leaving me in no doubt about her affection for me, she assured me she'd be allowed to visit me in a professional capacity, inside federal prisons, and so on and so on. She'd follow me even if the mission went badly—that was the subtext of what she was telling me. But she refused to get carried away by the romance of the situation and immediately switched back to interrogating me about what was being plotted, about the preparations for this riot. I immured myself in silence and moodiness; women love brooding men. The talentless actor Johnny Depp has sold billions of posters solely on the basis of his brooding good looks. She questioned me, but I avoided all her interrogations, playing cat and mouse with her. I was a very mysterious mouse.

Edith knew that Butterfly assaulted me, and she wanted to know what role he would play in the upcoming events. He'd be playing the corpse! *I have no idea.*

But she wouldn't let it drop. She must be unstoppable in bed once she gets going. *You seriously want to take it in the neck for him after everything he's put you through?* She wasn't well-versed in the nuances of prison hierarchy.

If it wavn't him, it would be fomebody elfe. I wasn't ashamed. I pointed out to her that sexual sacrifice wasn't just the prerogative of bosses' secretaries. And I was willing to bet that a colossus sting was worse than a butterfly sting. She didn't understand my animal metaphor. *Butterfly hav an average white male penif, but Coloffuf probably comev from a long line of big prickf. I'm not faying that becauve I'm rafift, it'f got nothing to do with rafe, it'f juft geneticf.*

She was totally gobsmacked by my spot-on analysis.

Nowadays we're all so uncomfortable talking about race. But the real racism is wanting to make everything equal without recognizing any differences. Black people like math, Asians like sports, brown people like carpets, and white people like expanding their territory and exterminating everyone else. It's well documented.

And your cellmate, would you take a bullet for him? I hear you've been having an argument over some tattoo he did for you.

What a flirt, she was certainly taking the long way round to get me naked. She was pretending to want to see the work of art on my flesh so she could get a good eyeful of the curves of my body. *I can fyow you if you want!* I stood up, ready to take off my shirt and get the foreplay started.

No, wait!

Wait, wait, I'm not a tea bag, for fuck's sake! She was letting me steep a little too long for my liking, I was probably going to develop a bitter aftertaste.

Tell me if he's in danger!

I was getting annoyed. *Ftop afking me if I'm going to attack fomeone, I've told you everything I know, do you truft me or not?*

Testosterone was flowing to my head, I was expressing myself too strongly and banging on the desk. In less than two seconds, Fat Mireille showed up. *Yes, Mireille, everything's fine, we're all good.* Obviously Edith had to break up our meeting so as not to attract suspicion. And I went away once more without any affection.

I was chasing the dirty pigeons when my doves touched down. A robin perching on the fence watched us. It was beautiful, yellow, luminous. Gilbert came over to admire it as well, deciding that it was a goldfinch. What an idiot, everyone knows that robins are yellow. He stuck to his guns, but my stubbornness was stronger than his stupidity. *A robin iv a robin iv a robin.*

My pair of doves slipped between the chain links. Leaning over to offer them a few bread crumbs, I opened my hands. Eventually the female landed on my wrist. I could feel her beak pecking my palm. Keeping guard, the male stayed on the ground, close to her, picking up the crumbs she dropped. When we were called back inside, I chased away my visitor by waggling my fingers. I was feeling emotional. With the murder I was going to commit in the next few hours, we might be cooped up for a long time. *Goodbye, my dovev, we'll fee eafh other foon. Rhoo, rhoo, rhoo.*

Louis-Honoré was waiting for me in my cell. *Last day, fucker, tomorrow's your last day to pay, in case you've forgotten.*

You poor idiot, if only you knew what was coming.

No, I haven't forgotten anything. All my accountv will be fettled tomorrow, maybe even thif evening!

The feevning?

Sigh. *THIF! EVENING!*

Haha, sure, fucker, this evening.

When he worked out what I was saying, he seemed surprised and disappointed. You'd think he liked the idea of beating me up more than the idea of getting the money. But he wouldn't be getting cash or a fight. It was going to be child's play to cut the grass from under his feet and roll myself a joint with it.

Pedo went into his cell when Butterfly came back from the hole, just before the trays were collected. He took the last one and sat down, for the last time, next to Big Dick and Denis. I thought: *Warm up my spot, you jerk!* I was trembling but I was ready. Very subtly, I tapped the shank on my groin. All that was left to do was wait for the signal, wait and pounce, like wild hyenas in the jungle.

The scene was set; the shift changed at eight on the dot. Edith left the wing, Tony came back on duty. BANG! BANG! BANG! My heart was beating double time, ready, set, go. Fat Mireille signalled to Gilbert to follow her into the office for his follow-up meeting. BANG! BANG! Tony stationed himself in front of the guard's office, blocking the view of the entrance to the showers. BANG!

Denis nodded at Colossus. Colossus murmured in Timoune's ear. Timoune headed toward the showers and looked over at Butterfly. Butterfly got up from the table and followed him…

Big Dick smiled at me.

My heart was leaping between my throat and my guts like a yo-yo on speed. I was walking, but it was like I was subject to excessive gravity, it felt like crawling, my body was so heavy. Each step took an eternity. Time was stretching out like chewing gum under the July sun. I had to go and meet my destiny, but an unknown force was holding me back, stopping me from moving forward. I noticed Tony's panicked eyes as he stood by the box. With all his silence, he was yelling at me to turn around, not to go into the showers, not to go in there with Timoune and Butterfly. He was a mere grain of salt in the cogs of this assassin; I could hear neither his distress nor the unknown energy that you might, I suppose, call conscience. I had a date with history.

It was all over in a few seconds. As soon as I turned the corner into the showers, I realized Butterfly had been lured there by a drug deal. You don't need honey to attract flies to shit. Leaning over a washbasin, with the outer section of a ballpoint pen in his hand, he was getting ready to snort a line of powder. With an old druggie's reflex, I lost a precious nanosecond wondering what substance it was and how to get hold of some. Next to him, Timoune was giving me a scornful look, amazed that I'd dared to join them. I needed to act quickly. If I took the blade out of my underwear, Timoune might think I wanted to lay into him and might block me. If I didn't make the most of Butterfly being distracted, he might get the upper hand. Action!

Intelligence put into action bypasses reflection. There's a proverb about that: *carpe diem*. It's of Latino origin. It means make the most of it while it's there.

Counting on the effect of surprise, I ran the three steps between me and Butterfly. Timoune leapt backwards, astounded.

When I reached my victim, I jumped and brandished my two fists in the air and let myself fall with all my weight, hitting Butterfly's skull with both fists. *Kapow!* I still wonder if he had time to snort the line.

Just as I'd hoped, the plastic tube had plunged through his nasal wall, his sinuses, his prefrontal lobe, and then got stuck in his corpus callosum. In other words, Butterfly had a pen jammed in his brain. But instead of dropping dead or at least dropping to the ground, he leapt suddenly to his feet and started to yell like a pig with its throat being cut. A pig with incredible vocal cords.

Frrrrroooouuuuuuuuiiithhh! His eyes rolled back in his head, which he was shaking in all directions, beating the air with his arms, Butterfly wanted to fly away. He was twisted with pain, his face frozen into a simian grimace. Oh my God, I thought. *Oh my God*, I said. It was pretty terrifying.

Timoune was swearing in Creole, pressed up against the wall, kneading the floor with his feet as if he wanted to sink into it. He was in shock. I was seriously disturbed, Butterfly was too agitated to be properly stabbed, the whole wing must have heard his screeching right out of the ninth circle of hell. The cavalry would be arriving any minute. What should I do?

I grabbed the shiv out of my tighty whities and threw it at Timoune as hard as I could. Black guys have excellent reflexes, it's all down to their intergenerational sporty genes, that's totally scientific and well documented. Timoune had excellent reflexes. He caught the weapon I'd just thrown, shouted like some sissy with PTSD, then dropped the weapon on the floor.

I chanced one last look at Butterfly. His body was covered with blood, which was pissing out of his nose in great floods. He was emptying fast. I raced out, crashing into Tony, who was on his way in, and I yelled at the top of my lungs, *Timoune killed Butterfly, fucking hell, guys, Timoune's killed Butterfly!*

9

DISCRETION

In the isolation cell, in the hole, the only company I had was graffiti. Since we are relieved of our belts and laces, I guess it was all carved with fingernails or dentures. Even if you've already read them a thousand times, you read them again, just to pass the time and recognize the artists' talent.

Your mother blows... Prison iz all in ur head... Seven yeers left to go... Christian Mistral was here... Fuck Fat Mireille... Black Power fucks yo mama... Life's a bitch... and tons of pictures: hearts, knives, women's bodies, and birds.

Since I was the main witness and a secondary suspect in the attack on Butterfly, I got put in the hole for a week while the police investigated. The two inspectors on my case were young and buff. They could have been police striporams! It's kinda pointless having big muscles when you have a gun, but I think being ripped made them feel good about themselves. Bodybuilding is very homosexual.

I had to meet Detective Jalbert and Detective Vivier, young men in their thirties, but old-school police officers. Jalbert played good cop and Vivier played bad cop. It was cute. I was going to fool them with one hand up each of their asses. Or tied behind my back, whatever turns you on.

I stuck to the basic story: I showed up in the showers, Timoune was holding a knife in his hand and attacking Butterfly. I didn't really see what was going on, they were wrestling each other. *No, I don't know what he hit him with. Yef, he had the knife in his handv. No, I have nothing againft Butterfly perfonally. Yef, I saw Timoune attacking him with my own eyev. No, I didn't jump on Butterfly. No, I wasn't in on it.* For everything else, I stuck to the basic principle of every criminal worthy of the name: deny deny deny. I mean, it should hardly be up to us to provide all the evidence!

I guessed from the questions they asked that my victim was dead, or unconscious. They had Timoune's version, claiming he hadn't been the attacker. But they also had Tony's version, which corroborated mine. As the meetings went on, I learned that they'd got fingerprints off the blade. Timoune's, obviously. Well caught, dude!

It looked like plain sailing from here on, all I had to do was hold my course, blow some lies into the sails, and wait to be taken back to my wing. No longer just a simple inmate, but as Big Dick's lieutenant.

A whole week in a prison inside a prison is a long time. I didn't have visitors usually, but I mingled with the other inmates and my beautiful Edith, and the other guards could be entertaining too. In the hole all I could do was resist the police questioning and jerk off. That got annoying. After a week of boredom, she came to visit me.

Edith confirmed that I'd be allowed back to my cell before too long.

I've been thinking a lot about you. I miff our meetingv.

She'd changed, I think the murder had rattled her, she was serious. *You lied to me! You said that they were planning a riot. You knew Butterfly was in danger!*

No wonder they call them drama queens: drama is to women like honey is to bees, they produce and consume as much of it as possible.

I didn't lie to you, I told you what I knew. I warned you that fomething wav in the works, but I didn't know what. Thove black guyv tried to trap me.

Nervous, and worried for the man she loved, she murmured, *What have you got mixed up in?*

I reassured her. *Don't worry, I'm in control, I'm not micfed up in anything. They know it wav Timoune who did it, their plan screwed up…*

She went away without saying goodbye or touching me. She was angry. Perfect, it's good for young couples to bicker. Then you can apologize and have great make-up sex, a good hard loving fuck.

A woman is a treasure, a box that just wants to be forced open.

My two little piggies came back to question me one last time to see if they could squeeze anything else out of me. But I'm not a lemon, so they left empty-handed. While Jalbert tried to tempt me with the promise of putting a favourable note in my file if I gave them more details, Vivier stared at me and wanted to know what kind of relationship I had with Colossus, Big Dick, and even Tony. That put a bug in my ear: I'd have to inform the boss. Our corrupt officer was suspected by the police.

I held firm all morning. Before leaving, they took my fingerprints digitally again, and my picture, and asked me to take off my shirt so they could photograph my tattoo. I didn't pay any attention to their snorts of derision. Police officers know nothing about the ancestral art of samurai. They wouldn't recognize an authentic one if they met one, the jerks.

They let me go out at the end of the day. They got me out of the hole, then out of the secure isolation wing to take me back to my protected section, inside a maximum-security prison. I felt like a Russian doll.

10

ADMIRATION

Butterfly wouldn't be making out with anyone again. He was in a deep coma. It's less impressive than a murder, but he was definitely broken. He wasn't likely to try to fuck the Mafia again, or me. Kept alive artificially in some hospital in the city, Butterfly is going to cost the state even more than he did when he was inside. It's ridiculous, they should have finished him off instead of intubating him.

I was listening to Philippe with an air of detachment, but in my head there was a raging inferno. I was dreading Big Dick's reaction. Would I be promoted or punished? I was disappointed that Butterfly wasn't dead, and I couldn't hide it. *But, man, who gives a shit if he's not dead, it's the same thing. You stabbed him in the brain with a pen. You're a warrior, man, you're fucking sick.* Philippe's compliments boosted my morale.

I really hoped it would be enough to make the Italians, the valued sponsors, and Big Dick happy at the same time. I hadn't had a chance to talk to him again, he and Denis were pretending to ignore me since I'd got back to the section. I assumed they were protecting themselves; welcoming me officially as one of their own would have confirmed the plot we were suspected of.

All the same, I'd hoped for a warmer welcome, not a guard of honour but some kind of recognition. But it was glacial: the agents on the floor underlined their suspicions by giving me the stink eye, while Colossus and Louis-Honoré were machine-gunning me with their stares, and Gilbert and Pedo wouldn't even deign to stop watching a *Deal or No Deal* rerun. Philippe was the only one to be amazed. So that was something.

Man, I can't get over it! It was a major deal this week, we all got interviewed like ten times, and we had police in the wing every day. Totally crazy! My new lawyer told me Timoune's been charged with attempted murder. There's gonna be a big trial—that'll give us a chance to get out and about, we'll have to be witnesses.

It was a major deal for our section, but much less so in the real world. The media barely covered it, just a quick CBC item on safety in prisons, and on CTV a former inmate who had witnessed difficult living conditions. Global carried on broadcasting weight-loss contests for obese people between two episodes of *Dr. Phil*. A couple of short items in the newspaper. I was disappointed, I thought it would have made more noise. But I guess violence in prison is more common than a toothless whore. And Big Dick's territory wasn't exactly big news.

I promised myself I'd make people talk about me in the future. For now, though, anonymity was useful. The people who needed to know knew. Word was getting around in the prison, and in other prisons too. If I was transferred, I would find the same notoriety somewhere else. My attack had turned out to be less prestigious than a murder by the book, but the initiative and the strength used would polish my reputation.

I had my first confirmation of this when I bumped into Denis as the dinner trays were being collected. He gave me his first nod, up and down, a greeting. Finally some recognition! It's not just the Scouts that earn their stripes if they work hard enough. But unlike a Scout, I'd never be abused again.

I still had to sit with the commoners, sharing a table with Gilbert and Philippe. I was chewing the chunks of rubber they called chicken breast when Gilbert spoke to me. *I have a message for you.* He was nervous and whispering, his head inclined toward me, which produced the exact opposite effect from the one he intended. More alert than ever, the guards noticed, and Dany started heading straight over to us. *Wait!* We went back to our plates and our plastic cutlery, which seemed to have become permanent. The guard prowled around our table a few times to really show us that he knew there was something shady going down. But when you have a long sentence to serve, there's not much else to do except be patient.

Once the warden had gone away, Gilbert broke the silence and turned back toward me. Anxiously I waited for him to pass on a threat from Colossus, or tell me that Butterfly had woken up. *Big Dick wants me to tell you your debt's taken care of.* I turned to look at Big Dick, who was ignoring me, and then toward Colossus, who was boring his evil eye into me. Well, well, well. I was all settled up. Who's laughing now? Who's laughing with a nice free tattoo on his skin? I took another mouthful of the chicken, which wasn't so bad, after all. Gilbert finished the message: *You're not in debt to Colossus anymore, but you haven't finished your contract… You're still in debt to Big Dick!* That certainly threw a plastic fork in the works.

A pig that isn't fully grown is called a piglet. Tony the piglet must have failed the intelligence test for joining the police. It probably asked him to count to twenty. Whatever the exam asked, he obviously screwed up. Hence his pathetic job as guard. His muscles were up to the task, I admit, but he didn't even come up to my brain's ankle. Even if he had been my accomplice in the attack on Butterfly, I was going to set him straight on a few things.

While all my associates were jostling to get out and take their daily puff of air, I hung back in the doorway. As soon as the coast was clear, I approached my rival. Our face-to-face chat might swerve into a faceoff. I was going to inform him that my woman was not polygamous.

I can fee right through your little game, piglet!

Tony smiled at me, intimidated.

Laft Thurvday, onfe again, one time too many, you were beating a dead one!

His smile faded. *A dead what?* You *need to stop beating around the bush. Say what you mean!*

Prison's a bad place to play the innocent. *I faw you trying to fedufe Edith, with your little fmilev and your little mufflef, fo juft ftop it!*

He wasn't just laughing anymore, he was honking with laughter. *Hahaha! If you think I want to bang Edith, you're even more out of it than I thought!*

His trick didn't throw me. *I'm not the one who's going to be out of it, you're the one who's going to be out of it, little piggie!* I have an awesome punch, just like Muhammad Ali.

His voice turned vicious. I was expecting that: like all animals, men become aggressive when they are afraid. *Don't you threaten me, you little shit! I don't give a fuck about your Edith, nor about you, so change your tone fast!*

The muscular right arm he was hitting my chest with didn't impress me much. *I don't give a fuck about you either. But don't forget that I have fome informaffion on you, you piglet!*

Leaving the door open, he moved to where we couldn't be seen and pushed me up against the wall. *Who the fuck do you think you are? You understand absolutely nothing about anything going on inside. You know nothing about me or about what I do. I'm going to give you a piece of advice: suck it up and don't ever threaten me again.* He'd understood the message. I had nothing to add.

As he was grabbing me by the neck to push me out into the yard, I realized that he and I would end up duking it out. I hated him so much. He had a finger in too many pies and he was pissing in my sandbox. His entire being was crying out for a violent death.

In the yard everyone was going about their usual business, minus Butterfly and Timoune. Nobody dared touch my victim's training bench. His weights were still on the bar. Only Louis-Honoré was strong enough to lift that much, but he was tucked away in a corner of the yard with his boss, dreaming up some scheme or other.

In the other corner I found my doves. It's wrong to use the expression "birdbrain." These mourning doves remembered me, unlike my mother, that damn bitch I'd love forever. My little couple were waiting for me, along with a third, more nervous dove, which stood to one side. I chased away a nuthatch with the back of my hand and then watched my animals feeding themselves from the hollows of my palms. This time it was the male who perched on my wrist, sticking his dry feet on my forearm. It tickled, but I was happy he was there. One day soon, both of my winged lovers would climb onto my arms to eat out of my hands. The moment would come.

I had to leave the last few crumbs on the ground and go back to my cell. Another search was starting—the prison wanted to keep the pressure on. The pressure was already too high. It was going to blow up in their faces, the jerks.

Our happiness reveals its fullest flavour only when confronted with other people's jealousy. Fries are good, but they're even better with ketchup. I liked it when Philippe questioned me about the plots underway, what I thought I might do with my new rank, what concrete benefits this new status had brought me. *Well, ftraightaway I have the right to get tattoov without going through Coloffuf.*

He frowned. *I don't think so… Seriously, if you want me to work on your knight, you have to go through him.*

It'f not a knight, it'f a famurai, I ranted.

He smiled. *Yes, sorry, that's what I meant. Anyway, it's gonna be hard to get another machine in here. They took away a package of mine too. They don't want me to have access to pens anymore… thanks to you! I'll have to use a mixture of ash and oil, it's not easy.*

I wasn't impressed. *I don't have to go through Coloffuf, I'm a free avent, for one thing. And for a fecond thing, you meffed up my famurai, even the fucking polife thought it wav funny. Fo you owe me a tattoo, that'f all!* I was getting carried away, he didn't dare answer anymore. *Fo maybe you'll do me a tattoo tonight, for free. You fay you're good at lettering, so you can do a tattoo on my forearm in nife gothic letterv.*

Philippe looked stunned and lost. It was almost endearing. He was scrambling for a way to deflect, evade, or otherwise avoid angering me while also not attracting Colossus's ire. *I can't, I have to talk to him first.*

I thumped the mattress with my fist. *No, I'm in Big Dick'f gang now, I have prefedenfe over Coloffuf!*

His face changed into a question mark. You have what?

I sighed, full of condescension. *I have prefedenfe, that meanv that I come before him, you ffould read more!*

He didn't want to talk literature and just contented himself with warning me of his intentions. *I'm gonna tell Colossus you forced me.*

I laughed. *Fure, go ahead, that'll give him a bone to gnaw on.*

Still perturbed, he got up to collect the pieces of the machine from their hiding places all over the cell.

The most important thing for respect is being feared. It's a guarantee. A good weapon is always more impressive than a good argument. If any old ass-licker could stop respecting you from one day to the next, you don't have a foundation for building your empire. I wasn't just some Sunday entrepreneur taking it one day at a time, I wanted to build big. It was essential to make him understand.

While he was putting his machine together, I repeated a new chorus from my next album, my first. *Fuck yeah! There's a new motherfucker in town, fuckers. Fuck yeah! Don't try to fuck me or I'll fuck you hard as fuck, fuck yeah!* It's crazy how much better it sounds in English. But I'll have to keep some French in so I'm eligible for grants.

11

FAITHFULNESS

Even though my hand had had a chance to do some pole dancing, I was still stressed that morning. The criminal hierarchy ladder has greased rungs. Aware that my position was still precarious, I was hemming and hawing about what attitude to take. Should I stand up to the black guys? Should I show clemency to Philippe? And above all, how could I supplant Denis and get close to the leader of my gang? As for Edith, could I be open about our relationship without putting her in danger or attracting her colleagues' hostility?

Social behaviour is complicated for human beings. I've always been rejected because I was kind and misunderstood, so I haven't learned all the codes and customs. For my entire childhood, I moved between foster families and group homes, always shunted along before I could grow roots, so I always plateaued at first contact. When there was first contact. It's pretty hard to improve your social skills alone in your corner.

At least in a criminal milieu, people live as they die, with firm codes: money, the omertà, and the settling of accounts. That clarifies certain grey areas. Reputation's important too, but precarious. On that point, I knew I was making progress. Any show of aggression wins you points. I could see that just from the way my cellmate looked at me.

The Sage had started looking at me differently. His gaze tunnelled into the depths of my soul and analyzed every feature of my face, before concluding: *I just can't fucking believe you did that. You jammed a pen in his head?*

Shhh, shhh. I ordered him in a whisper to talk less loudly. Dany, the warden on duty, was pretending to look through the cartoons section. I knew his ears were twitching to hear and he'd have taken malicious pleasure in seeing me go down. *Obvioufly I can't confirm anything, but you're a librarian, furely you can read between the linev…*

The Sage nodded his head deferentially. It was a real shame he was going to die soon. I liked my librarian. Especially his way of looking at me, of taking the time to talk to me and find me interesting. What other people think about us is important, it determines how we think about ourselves.

A pen in his fucking brain, I've seen everything now.

Shhh… It wav juft the outfide of the pen, there wavn't any ink left…

Yeah, sure, that changes everything. Ha, you're a real comedian!

The guard was approaching, we had to change the subject fast.

I asked him to recommend me an adventure book, but he wanted to drone on about his damn poetry again. *I already know who Leonard Cohen iv, give it a reft!* He was just some Montreal lyricist who found fame late in life. Now Bryan Adams and Gordon Lightfoot and all those singers just copy him. Back when he was reading his own songs, he didn't even have any musicians to accompany him. Posthumous glory is only good for the heirs.

The Sage pressed the point, swore to me that he was more than just a lyricist, that I absolutely had to read *Wonderful Losers*, his masterpiece. I took the book to make him happy.

Poets are even lazier than prisoners. They don't even fill a quarter of a page, it's all a big fraud. I wanted some real reading, so I searched for myself. I took out *The Secret* for the fourth time. With the firm intention of finishing it. Then I found myself a fantasy novel about knights with dragons and magic, which is always good. The clue's in the name: it's fantastic.

Before I left, with my books under my arm like a schoolgirl in uniform, with her sheer black stockings pulled up to her knees, showing some thigh under the hem of her green-and-navy-checked skirt, which concealed pristine cotton underwear…I heard the Sage call me. *One day I'll understand who you are, who you really are.*

The guard turned toward us, intrigued, waiting for my reply. *I don't think anyone will ever really know who I am, maybe not even myfelf.* And I left without waiting, proud of myself, with the guard at my heels.

Colossus waltzed into my cell like he owned the place, or so I imagine, having never owned a place myself. When I saw him coming I hoped against hope he was coming to meet Philippe. But no. The moment of confrontation had arrived. I abandoned my scientific reading on the laws of attraction and got up to face him. The tension was high. Philippe vanished quicker than a bag of powder up Ozzy Osbourne's nose. Colossus grabbed me by the forearm, staring at my new tattoo. I let him do it, wanting to figure out which side he was going to attack from.

With his gravelly voice, he spelled out T-I-E-D-H. He lifted his head and, a smile twitching at the corners, asked me how long I'd been in love with Edith. The bastard, he was good. I'd been so sure that none of the idiots in the wing would manage to figure out my anagram. *No idea what you're talking about. I don't give a ffffit about Edith.*

His smile grew but his contempt didn't change. He didn't let go of my arm, and even grabbed my wrist harder. "What da fuck? You think I don't clock what yo dilly?"

I really should learn more slang, it would be trill handy for business conversations in prison.

We have an agreement with your boss for the shit on your back, fucker, but from now on nothing goes ahead without my say-so, that's the deal. Get it?

Even though I was trembling, and his fingers digging into my skin were making me think of the great Christian martyrs, I didn't let him intimidate me.

Furely we can talk about thif man to man and have a—
THWACK!

He hit me with the back of his hand, getting a good smack to the jaw. I wanted to roll over on my bed and curl up, but he didn't let my arm go and held me upright. *Stop trying to fool me, you fucker. You're not a man, you're just a pawn, a fucking pawn, do you understand? We don't want to see the po-po back here again, that's the only thing stopping me from smashing your head in. You have nothing, I know, nothing to pay me and nothing to offer! I'm gonna negotiate with Denis, but don't you ever ask my tattooer to do anything again. Don't ever go over my head again!*

See, I knew we'd end up getting along, he just had to ask Denis, my immediate superior, to pay him, no need to make a big song and dance about it.

That'f fine by me, Coloffus, fine by me!

He gripped my arm one last time. It worked out okay because I'd already crossed my pain threshold. *You don't call me Colossus, asshole! You don't call me anything, nothing at all, don't ever speak to me!*

Nonetheless I told him to have a nice day and didn't keep him.

Black guys are good negotiators. That's why they control the drug retail market and street whores. They're good with people. Any day now they'll be taking over the entire global economy!

My lawyer couldn't get over my being involved in a second aggravated assault in less than a year. I pointed out that, unlike the crazy cat lady in Sherbrooke, Butterfly wasn't dead. And that theoretically I wasn't even responsible for the attack on Butterfly. He quickly brought me back down to earth with a bump—no, make that a punch in the gut. The charges being brought against Timoune could easily be brought against me; not only did Timoune continue to insist that I was the only one responsible, but also—and here he spoke with emphasis—Carol might wake up. I burst out with a nervous laugh. Over time I'd forgotten that Butterfly's real name was Carol. My laughter became forced, and then panicky. He might wake up?

My lawyer had pressed the right button. Seeing the worry spread across my face, he merely sighed. *Yep, that's what I thought, you are mixed up in this shit, and now it's deep shit. Not only might he wake up, but he's stable and actually has more brain activity than they thought.*

I was stunned. Butterfly had brain activity? Remembering suddenly that he was my ally and was supposed to support me, the lawyer tried to be reassuring. *There's no sign of him waking up for now, he's in a coma, but he's out of mortal danger. Nobody has any idea what could happen.*

If he regained consciousness, my entire criminal career would be compromised. Even with a hole in his skull, that ass fucker was still threatening me!

It was turning out to be a total bad-news day. First the possibility of my lepidopteran returning to consciousness, as well as the torture of seeing Edith ignore me and cancel our meetings, and on top of that, new crazies were arriving in our wing. Nature abhors a vacuum, and we had plenty of nature red in tail and claw in our cell block. With the prison occupation rate approaching 140 per cent, I knew that the places freed up by Timoune and Butterfly would soon be filled, but it was still upsetting.

There's no such thing as chance. Especially in prison. Everything is counted, from the cutlery to the minutes in the visiting room to the group dynamics of each wing. The prison leadership had the power to alter the fragile balance of our microsociety. I could define the unstable power relationships in terms of chess. Chess is intelligent, like Russians. Russian women are blond, hot, and sensual, and they basically just wear black lingerie, this is well documented on the Internet and in specialist magazines. But I'm getting distracted—back to chess; black versus white, you're already getting the picture.

On one side we had Colossus, the black king, who had a powerful rook in Louis-Honoré and a pawn named Philippe the Filipino. Opposite, King Big Dick still had the upper hand, supported by a knight and a bishop. Smack my bishop, as the Prodigy sang, was a perfect fit for Denis, with his all-seeing gaze and excellent connections. As for me, the knight, I still hoped to make a conquest of Queen Edith and surprise everyone with a timely sidestep.

They could have tried to keep the existing balance. But since they had the chance to shuffle the cards—and the cages—they took it. Instead of bringing in reinforcements for the two existing gangs, they chose instead to swell the ranks of Pedo's clan. And they didn't just bring in two replacement crazies—filling the space left by Giuseppe too, they brought in three in one go.

Why make something easy when you can make it complicated? With this generous addition to our wing, which was already on the point of exploding, the management destroyed morale. This new Holy Trinity of morons was made up of Beanpole, Melon, and mathieu. It's important to use the right words: unbearable parasites sounds weak, but it's the only thing coming to mind. We'd need to ask a writer. Or a dictionary of synonyms.

The tall skinny guy was the most seriously affected, he was as stupid as a Czech ballet. And they put him in a cell with Pedo. The worst that could happen was that they'd drool on each other and invent a primitive language. Poor Beanpole, another victim of overmedication. He was a long way from being a schizophrenic in remission—in fact, you only had to mention Jesus and he broke out in a sweat. Whenever he was getting on our nerves, we brought up Satan. That's all it took to make him run back to his cell, where he intoned a hundred *Our Fathers* to recover.

He was twenty-two and had no name at all, we didn't care, we just called him Beanpole, and he doesn't even deserve your attention. He's not important in this story, and he's not the one I killed.

The second reinforcement, the big Melon, was called Steven and claimed he had Indigenous ancestry. What a liar: he had an American first name, his obesity was down to American junk food, he'd shot his wife with an American rifle, and he was an evangelical Christian. Humming along to Kashtin or buying a dream catcher isn't enough to lay claim to a many-thousand-year-old culture.

And he had a squint! Have you ever heard of an honest man with a squint? It's not well documented though. Some university ought to waste taxpayers' money on researching it.

Steven, the pudgy melon, stank, which was an important detail in this confined environment. Some people smell like swing. He was worse: he reeked of jazz. He never spoke and was always laughing to himself for no reason. But I sniffed out his hypocrisy right away. He'll be less of a smartass when I shove a knife into his ribs.

Last and most definitely least came mathieu, no capital letter. A drifter who took a wrong turn. Prison is full of sons of bitches, but the authorities don't allow any dogs. And a young guy on the streets without a dog is lost. He was so anxious and introverted that he never even lifted his head. Poor kid, that wasn't enough to let him go unnoticed. The very day of his arrival, I heard Louis-Honoré calling dibs on him. We could hear him moaning morning and night. Luckily for him, Louis-Honoré was speedy with his little peashooter, which limited the damage.

Little mathieu attempted suicide a few times during his stay with us. In my opinion, you might as well kill someone else as yourself. Your attacker, let's say. But mathieu had fewer balls than a eunuch. Or at least that's what he let us believe when he arrived. Another hypocrite whom I'll make pay for it one day.

I was listening to Melon jerking off on my right when Denis came and stood under the shower to my left. Denis wore black lycra swim shorts in the showers, Ocean Mist brand with fuchsia stripes on the sides, very tight. He was never without his swim shorts. He must have been saddled with some little embarrassment, I guess. Heteromasculine intimacy doesn't turn every inmate on.

I didn't dare speak to him, but I dragged out the washing process so I could stay beside him. He was pretty charismatic, and I rarely had the chance to be close to one of my fellow gang members. I was washing my armpits for the third time when he spoke to me. *Tomorrow…*

I jumped and dropped the soap. Melon thought that was funny; I threatened him with my fist to show him it wasn't. He laughed anyway. I picked up my little bar of soap and stood back under the shower. Denis, annoyed, started up again on his long-winded speech. *Tomorrow at dinner, you're going to sit with us.*

Finally! July was almost over; three weeks had melted away since I'd cut Butterfly's wings off.

Yef, yef, I'll come and fit with you.

Denis was warming up his voice. *We need you. It's something bigger this time. Stay ready.*

Bigger than Butterfly? Did they want me to tear Colossus limb from limb with my teeth? *I'm ready for anything, Denis!* I was so excited I could have hugged him. But I don't think he would have been comfortable with that in the showers. Instead, I soaped myself up vigorously, smiling to infinity and beyond.

12

THE PARDON

Edith wanted to make up. It was about time! She'd been sulking with me for almost a month, which wasn't serious, even for a woman. I showed up to our meeting with a flower. A paper flower. Even if it was a fake flower, women like the thought that counts.

What is it? she said, as if she couldn't tell what it was. She's very playful, my Edith.

It'f a flower, a paper flower. It'f like love, it doevn't fade.

She twirled it on its stem for a moment. *Thank you. It's the thought that counts.*

Bingo! Ten points to me.

I'm going to be honest with you. I feel like you lied to me. I don't know how much you were involved in the attack on Butterfly, but you weren't there for no reason. Especially as you claimed to know that there was a plan that involved you. You should never have been there.

I put on my innocent little virgin face. *I wav juft there by chanfe, Edith.* I wanted to tell her the truth, to be open and honest, tell her the whole story. But all the beauty of impossible love stories lies in those shady zones. *I didn't do anything! I fwear, Edith, you have to believe me, I only have you to tell the truth to!*

Her expression softened. *I don't know if I should believe you. The other agents think Big Dick set the whole thing up, that it wasn't Timoune who did it but you.*

I suspected that the screws suspected me. *No, no, tell them, you have to ftand up for me, Edith, we truft eacfh other. You promifed me!*

She didn't let me take her hand. *No, hang on, I didn't promise anything.*

I insisted. *But truft iv a promife…*

I wasn't expecting her to stand up and flaunt her enormous hips. Even seen from the front, she had a big ass.

What was Denis saying to you in the showers yesterday? Why did you sit with Big Dick at lunch? Don't take me for an idiot, I know you're working for them now.

I was disconcerted. How could she have known that Denis had invited me to lunch while we were in the showers? Was Melon a double agent? I had to speak to the boss, and fast. Maybe we were bugged.

Egvactly, Denif invited me to eat with them, that'f all. I think they were lonely, he and Dzilles.

She burst out laughing. *Give it a rest with your "Gilles." You can't tell me that Big Dick just wanted to hang out with you instead of that goon, what are you doing for him?*

I needed to give her a crumb before she snatched the whole loaf away from me. Sometimes you need to sacrifice a small truth to hide a larger one.

I juft give him my medicafion, that'f all.

She paused and wilted a little. *I suspected as much, but I'm sure that's not the whole story.*

I rearranged my face into an expression of repentance. *Yef, Edith, I fwear, I'm doing nothing wrong.*

Like a slab of veal beneath the hammer of fine words, she became more tender. *And what's this tattoo?*

I'd let my arm rest on the desk in full view, hoping that she would see right through the chaos, that it would take her breath away, that she'd walk around the desk and finally consummate our passion. *You do know I could send you straight to the hole for that, nobody's allowed to get a tattoo inside these walls, and now you've done it twice.*

There was still some gristle left in her steak. *But I had no choife, EDITH, if I wanted to furvive infide I had to get theve letterf written on my fkin. It reminds me of fomeone very important to me…*

She remained unmoved. *I don't know why you'd be stupid enough to get a tattoo, but for now, the only name you should be focusing on is your own. What with the company you're keeping and Jocelyn having you in his sights, along with everything else going on in this wing, you should just be thinking about protecting yourself.*

All women are mothers deep down. Even those whose uteruses are useless or unused. They always want to protect the ones they love, the one they love.

I reassured her, promised her I'd take care, if only for her sake, but Edith was already opening the office door wide and asking me to leave. She wanted to carry on playing, draw out the pleasure, let me stew in my desire. *The higher you jump, the harder you fall*, as James Dean murmured in an excellent film I've never seen. I had lots of momentum. I was going to hit it hard when the time came.

As it happens, there was no reason for Edith to make a meal out of my team lunch. I was expecting to be entrusted with an important mission, to chat business or to undergo a rite of passage. But life is a letdown, and humans take pride in being disappointing. Denis made me sit down between him and Big Dick, then they ate in silence. For a long time. As if nothing was up. I suppose it was just to show me off, let people know I was one of theirs. So at least there was that.

I looked around between two mouthfuls of stew, savouring the other inmates' jealous looks. Especially Colossus and Louis-Honoré. I didn't dare imagine what they'd give to be sitting right in the spot occupied by my little white ass. Some people might have thought they were glaring at me aggressively, or even with hatred, but an analyst like me knows how to spot jealousy under the frowning brows.

I was picking my bottom teeth with a fork when Denis broke the silence, imbued with the solemnity of Christ breaking the host. *From now on, you're going to eat with us two, you're going to talk to me alone, and you're not going to do any more tattooing nonsense or anything else. Got it?*

Yef, but…

No buts. Denis signalled that I shouldn't add anything. Big Dick didn't add anything either, adjourning our first official meeting with his last mouthful of pudding.

I hoped the library would have a copy of the Karma Sutra. We can barely get any porn in prison. It's unacceptable, it ought to be considered a basic right for all men from the age of twelve all the way to death. I told myself that with the famous Indian sports manual in my hands I'd at least be able to stimulate my imagination. But no, Fat Mireille and I walked all the way along the two endless corridors for nothing.

The library was closed because the librarian was being evaluated by the parole board to see if he could get early release. My chunky escort swore as she tried to catch her breath. I hoped they'd refuse to liberate the Sage. He was the only member of my book club. And we'd become friends over the months; you can't be disliked by everyone. Sometimes he recommended interesting books to me. He explained the plots I didn't get, and corrected me when I quoted the wrong author, which rarely happened. But most of all he listened to me and never insulted me. And that's not nothing. I really liked him; I could only wish that his hopes would be dashed.

On the way back, Mireille asked me if she could see my base-ball tattoo. I told her to take a hike and pointed out my skin was decorated with a samurai, not a batter. She apologized but insisted on seeing it, she'd been assured that it was worth it. But she was wasting her breath. I wasn't going to get undressed just to satisfy some obese old woman's curiosity, and I wouldn't fail to denounce her to her colleague. Sparks would fly when Edith heard Mireille had been trying to turn her man in to a stripper.

Back in my wing, I immediately noticed that something was off. It wasn't Beanpole on all fours and patting the floor. It wasn't the turned-off TV. It was the peace and quiet, rarer than fair-trade cocaine. There was a monastic silence. Only Pedo and Beanpole were in the common area.

Dany, the guard who'd recommended my dorsal master-piece to his colleague, cast a distracted glance at the crazies. Why was everyone in their cells? More cunning than Geronimo himself, I gave Mireille the slip and sneaked over to my own cell. Bingo! I could hear whispering. To avoid attracting attention, I pressed myself up against the wall, a few inches away from the door frame, pretending to clean my nails. I was trying to be more discreet than a fruit-fly turd.

I struggled to make out all the voices. I recognized Philippe, the current tenant. I was amazed to hear a voice I didn't recognize. Then I identified the third as Colossus. But the second one wasn't Louis-Honoré. Then the mysterious man snickered. It was Melon! I recognized that hideous cackle from the showers. Here was the evidence: not only was he pretending to be a non-verbal crazy, he was also a double agent—or, who knows, maybe even a triple agent—working both for the prison and for Colossus. This was a plot twist straight out of the best kind of novel!

I was burning with impatience to report this intel back to Big Dick. Going through Denis, obviously. They'd be so proud of me, maybe they'd even touch me. I was hoping for a pat on the back, but I'd be happy with a handshake. But for now, at risk of bursting, the balloon of my surprise was getting strained. They were still talking.

The big traitor was talking about managing the hooch and bringing all substances under one system. Philippe replied that with a monopoly they could inflate the prices as much as they wanted. Colossus mumbled some vernacular Creole phrase before ending by whispering, *We'll have free run once Big Dick's gone.* I was having heart palpitations. This was a serious plot, they were legit going to take out the head of my organization.

I had enough information to run to my gang's HQ cell. But curiosity and my weak legs kept me pinned to the wall for a few seconds longer. A few nearly fatal seconds. Colossus was talking about September being a time of reorganization when Louis-Honoré came out of the cell and stood right in front of me.

By the grace of God and fashion, Louis-Honoré was concentrating on shifting the elastic waistband of his jogging pants lower down on his ass. Since he had his head bent down during this operation, it gave me the time to take three quick steps backwards. Very subtly, I then started moving back toward my cell while singing that old Sex Pistols hit: *Clang clang go the jail guitar doors, Bang bang go... Oh! Sorry, Colossus. I didn't mean to disturb you.* I'd put on a relaxed look, but hardened criminals are suspicious by nature.

Colossus grabbed my neck. *What do you want, fool?*

Quick thinking. *Well… it if my fell.*

While Colossus was gripping my face just a few inches away from his, Louis-Honoré came into the cell and stood behind me, grabbing me by the neck for good measure. *Is there a problem, Colossus?*

I felt as squeezed as a peanut butter sandwich being sat on by Mireille. What with Philippe, the obese guy with the confusing identity, and the black guys holding me down by my neck, the tension was rising.

Asshole don't have no problem, right? Colossus said.

I accept that it's important to affirm your virility in an all-male environment, but I was starting to think that maybe Colossus didn't respect me enough. *No, no problem.*

I could breathe more easily once my Afro-Haitian assailants released me. It was just my cellmate left. Unlike his employers, he knew how to ask a question clearly. *Hey, man, do you think you heard something when you came in that it would have been better if you hadn't been here to hear?* Shakespeare would have beamed with pride.

Philippe's shot was on target but he didn't score a goal. I took possession of the ball again and ran back to the other end. *I didn't hear a thing, I wav finging a fong. But that wav a weird meeting, in our fell, what'f going on?*

Pretending to rummage in a drawer to avoid my perceptive gaze, he tried to shake me off. *No, no, it wasn't weird, Colossus was looking for somewhere to talk with Fat Melon. He gets these horse pills, you know. He's gonna have to give them to the black guys… Huge doses of Klonopin, the good stuff.*

I agreed. *Yeah, but I don't underftand why you were meeting here.*

In a final attempt to show off, Philippe insinuated that he was the mule, he had to keep his boss's medication and marijuana in our cell.

Yef, right, that makeffenfe. And a million winged pigs were getting ready to fly right out of the prison.

This was serious, and I had no biteable nails. My gang was under threat. I had a sense of belonging deep in my gut. I hadn't often had a chance to show it, but I had a real sense of family. Denis and Big Dick were my fathers and my brothers at the same time. In a family you have to stick together and fight to protect yourselves. Out of pure love, like the Hiltons, those famous boxers and Montreal hotel moguls.

I was holding back with all my strength—I didn't want to go bursting into my chief's cell and attract our enemies' attention. Aware that they were preparing to attack us, we'd be able to get our defence ready. The best defence is always attack, and we were pushed for time. I decided to wait for the evening meal to pass the whole thing on to Denis. Big Dick would be sitting right next to us so he'd know that the intel came from me, and I'd benefit from his gratitude. Charity begins in Rome, as Saint Francis of the Mafia also said.

Big Dick would entrust me with the mission to deal with the rebels. I was already thinking about how I'd do it. When and how to take Colossus out? In all probability, I'd also have to kill Louis-Honoré. And Melon? Even Philippe? It wouldn't be easy to wipe out a whole gang in one fell swoop.

At long last the dinner trolley rolled around. I left my dragon story and jumped out of bed to nab my food as it went by. I was the first one sitting at our table. Waiting for my colleagues. My colleagues who kept me waiting so long that my meat loaf was cold when I finally decided to start eating it.

I was lonely and getting lonelier. I waited until everyone else had taken their trays back, and then I took mine over and spoke to the guard, in full ventriloquist mode.

Where'v my fam?

Paul sniggered. *Your little friends are with their lawyers, where they've been for far too long, if you want my opinion.*

This was a bad time for them to be reviewing their cases. Louis-Honoré cracked the knuckles of his enormous hands to get my attention. I was isolated, and more vulnerable than an inebriated virgin at a biker party.

I fled to my cell, praying that our enemies wouldn't come and take me out. I resisted the desire to hide under the covers, and stayed on guard for more than an hour, watching the entrance to the wing. Eventually Jocelyn brought Denis back. I would have preferred to talk to Big Dick, but like a good soldier I'd deal with his right-hand man.

He was tucking back a lock of white hair when I threw myself at him. *Denif, Denif, I have to talk to you!*

He stepped to one side, ignoring me. Jocelyn hadn't missed it and started heading over to us. I had to be quick.

Denif, there'v a plot againft uf, come to my fell right now.

Jocelyn had reached us and now he could hear everything. Denis was walking determinedly to his cell, pretending not to notice me. Blocking his way, I tried to make him understand the seriousness of the situation one last time.

It'f important!

He stopped. *Not as important as shutting your mouth and going to bed!*

Laughter broke out in the common area. My proud heart shattered in my rib cage and spun off in all directions.

Even if you've been subjected to it since childhood, you

never get used to rejection and humiliation. Humans are social creatures, and even the most idiotic of us need brotherly contact from time to time. If the social element withers away, we're nothing but animals. Wounded animals.

To the sound of my fellow inmates' mockery, I went back to my cell, my head held high. My heart was in bits, my body trembling with fury, I was saving myself and saving face. People whistled at me, repeated Denis's words back at me, told me to go to back to my kennel. Before I fell onto my bed, I swung my fist at the armoured door and yelled out in rage, *Eat shit and die, the whole lot of you!*

Humans aren't my favourite animal.

13

LOYALTY

I dreamed about Edith again. The images were even more disturbing than the first time. I don't dare even write them here or people will think I'm some sort of deviant. Let's just say it involved chainsaws, an abandoned warehouse, five German shepherds, and some fancy lingerie.

I was still reflecting on my dream when the breakfast call sounded. *Breakfast!* Simple and efficient. This time there was a second cart wheeled around the wing, lower than the regular one. This cart had a toaster, bread, peanut butter, bowls, cereal, and milk. Cows' milk and very gluteny bread, which was a big problem for me and my delicate intestinal flora. I had made several official requests, but the prison stood its ground, closed to the idea of allowing kamut or soya. And they totally refused to give me any Cap'n Crunch either. Frustrated, I made myself three slices of toast and a big bowl of disgusting Frosted Flakes. *Grrrrrreat...*

Denis and Big Dick pretended not to notice that I'd fallen out with them. Since I didn't talk that much, anyway, I was going to have to work hard on my attitude. The meal was coming to an end, I wasn't done with sighing and muttering between every mouthful. I was thinking of spitting on my plate when Denis unclenched his teeth. *Put your things away at the same time as us and then follow us into the showers without saying a word.*

There, it wasn't so hard to figure out that we had to talk. People in the business world underestimate the importance of interpersonal communication.

The showers were still a strategic place to discuss important things. For one thing, we were sure there were no listening devices. For another, the guards were obliged to stay a respectful distance away from us, to respect the inmates' privacy. And third, you have to look people in the eye. I certainly had to do that at this meeting. Both my colleagues were wearing swim shorts, and the same style at that. Black lycra with a fuchsia stripe and everything. It was weird to see Big Dick in such a simple getup. I was the only one wearing just a penis. Butt naked. You might have said they were wearing suits, or even a uniform, especially with the way they flanked me on either side.

Under Jocelyn's hostile gaze, Big Dick didn't even bother pretending to wash. He started the water and turned toward me. *Why did you get Edith's name tattooed on your arm?*

It'f not Edith'f name! I was shouting without meaning to. I was annoyed, my trick hadn't gone unnoticed by anyone except for Edith! *It'f not an anagram, it'f an acroftic…*

You really think I'm gonna buy that?

It'f the truth, it'f the firft letterv of a contemporary poem by Leonard Cohen.

Right, that's interesting. What's the poem?

I can't quite remember the title…

But you can remember what you've had inked on your arm, right?

Yef, yef, ov courfe I remember… Territory… intimacy evoked… death heals. That'f it! I'd got myself out of that one!

Territory: intimacy evoked, death heals? I didn't know Cohen wrote that.

Quick, think of something. *Yef, it'f from hiv mafterpiefe* Beautiful Hoser.

Big Dick was getting annoyed. *Alright, let's stop messing around, you're not the only one here who's read a book, you know. We're prepared to give you a chance, but we need to talk seriously.*

He threw Denis a complicit look, the kind of look I'd like to receive one day. For now, I had to try everything to change the subject and impress Big Dick. He never spoke directly to me, so I had to seize the chance. *I overheard a converfafion yefterday, you won't believe what I heard!*

Denis interrupted me again; they weren't here to listen to what I had to say, but to give me another contract, the most important contract of my life. *You'd be better off shutting your piehole and opening your ears!*

If they got iced by Colossus and his merry psychopaths, I wouldn't get any benefits from the contract. *Yeah, but but firft I have to tell you that—*

Denis grabbed my throat. *Didn't anybody ever teach you to keep your fucking mouth shut?*

Jocelyn was running over from his observation post, overly keen to intervene. But Big Dick ordered Denis to let me go, so when Jocelyn showed up there was nothing to discipline. Big Dick told him sharply that correctional officers were not permitted to come so close to inmates in the showers. The guard took a few steps back and offered to escort me to my cell. I scornfully refused and faced Big Dick. I had to let him know about the plot even though the clock was ticking. Since we just had ten minutes per shower, we couldn't start adding long digressions to the day's business.

What I'm trying to tell you iv that Coloffuf wantf to kill you! I'd never heard Big Dick laugh before. It stretched out, long and large, bouncing and echoing around the shows. *Hahahaha*

hahahaha haha hoo ha...

I'm feriouf, I heard him fay that he'd be in control of our fec-tion by Feptember, that you were going to "leave." I mimed some exaggerated air quotes to make him understand.

He started guffawing again. He wiped away the water that was splashing his face and then enlightened me. *Colossus isn't a danger or an enemy. He's an employee!*

I don't believe it! Big Dick had plotted out the whole scheme from the start. Lord Almighty, every single thing! Colonel de Gaulle looked like a kindergartener next to him. There never had been any rival gangs in our wing. *I ftill can't believe it!*

Between Denis's chuckles, Big Dick explained that the Italians directed everything from the outside and he was in charge of everything inside, and everyone else was under him. He got a cut from the tattoos all the way through to the moonshine, via all the drug deals, whether pharmaceutical or not. The entire racial-tensions thing was a smokescreen to keep the guards busy as well as to increase pressure on new inmates.

Everything was decided in advance. Giuseppe's thrashing was ordered from outside and paid for by his victim's family. Butterfly's case was an internal purge. He was getting too doped up and knew too much about the external operations. Big Dick found him useful and would have kept him, but he went along with what the big boss wanted, the real chief above my chief, the capo de tutti capi.

My mind was in a whirl, I'd carried out a contract for the Mafia godfather, the legit el padrino of the French-speaking underworld of eastern North America. I was already a Mafia underling, a big shot, I just didn't know it yet!

It was such a great honour, I was having trouble breathing. Especially in all this steam. *I don't underftand, why did you afk me to do that? Why not Coloffuf or Timoune?*

Denis took over the story. *Timoune had become a problem*

too, snorting too much. We wanted to get rid of our crazy dogs, kill two birds with one stone. You were the stone. It was a good shot.

Breathlessly, I turned back to Big Dick. They were making my head spin.

So good that if you make a go of the next contract, you'll get a promotion, whatever prison or wing you're in. Even when you get out, you'll definitely end up being a hit man for the Italians.

My dream was coming true, in the showers, with two men in swim shorts. I was finally becoming an official member of the Mafia, with all that that meant in terms of recognition, brotherhood, and hope in life.

I was a Mafioso, I was down with the biggest organization on the planet. It's no accident that the underworld is called Le Milieu: it's the centre of the world. The TV news confirms it every night; all the politicians and journalists get excited about the economy, they don't talk about anything else. And the two most lucrative markets in the known universe are drug trafficking and weapons trafficking. This is well documented. And well paid.

Lost in my thoughts, puffed with pride, I shivered with unbearable happiness. I had to sit down in the shower to gather my thoughts.

Denis wasn't impressed. He said my position was ambiguous and ordered me to get up immediately. Jocelyn laughed cheerfully, only sorry that he couldn't take a photo. I inhaled a great puff of steam and stood up, watching Big Dick.

We still need you. It's going to cost me an arm and a leg, but the Italians can get me out of here in a chopper. Like they did at Saint-Jérôme prison, like they do in France! I'd never seen Big Dick excited, he was getting agitated. *But I have to be in the interior yard at the precise time.*

I pointed out that our yard was caged on all sides, even my doves had to slip in.

Well, obviously not our yard, the yard for the whole prison. So that means I need the guard to open three doors, from two different observation posts. We're gonna need a solid reason and that reason is going to be your correctional officer!

More vertigo, the same palpitations. *Edith?*

Yup, you're going to take Edith hostage for me.

Ah, the eternal dilemma of great men: love or glory? You can never have everything, even if you're ready for anything. Big Dick was still gesturing, I could see his lips moving, but I couldn't hear anything. I felt like Sophie in *Sophie's Choice*, I imagine, although I haven't read it yet. Anyway, I had to make a choice, a choice that would tear me apart more than giving birth to triplets. For now, I had to keep all doors open. I put on my best poker face so that Big Dick wouldn't notice anything.

Are you alright? You look a bit weird. Disappointed.

I needed to work on the poker face. I soaped my buttocks and pretended to be feeling sentimental to distract him. *I'm fine, I'm juft eager to get going with your orderv, but I wav juft thinking it would be quiet around here with you gone.* Well played!

But you'll be leaving too! Once I've taken off, you can release your hostage. Get ready for a bit of roughing up, those guards all stick together. But they'll transfer you pretty quickly. You're going to be a legend, young man, whatever prison they put you in!

That made me feel a bit better.

And I'll look out for you from a distance too, I'll be more useful to you outside than inside. He put his hand on my shoulder and massaged my courage. *If you help me get out of this fucking shithole, I'll owe you big time.* Big Dick's face was full of promises.

With tears in my eyes and fear in my stomach, I swore to him that I'd do it.

It's gonna be on the twenty-sixth of August. You already have a meeting with Edith, we checked. Tony will be on duty with her.

I wanted to tell him about my suspicions regarding our corrupt guard, but he rebuffed me.

Tony's still on our floor and on our side. His sister already dances for us, he can't risk being hung out to dry. Until then, keep quiet, don't start any shit, you have three weeks to make yourself a weapon. I have faith in you!

Jocelyn came up to tell us we'd gone over our ten-minute shower time and we had to get out. Big Dick ended the meeting with a small nod. Like a good soldier, I went out first. To send the dog sniffing along the wrong track, Denis yelled at me to pay my debts. *Next time we won't warn you first!*

I left the showers feeling happy but in despair. I would have to leave my sweetheart to get my heart's desire. Or sabotage my attempts at social climbing to stay close to her. Overwhelmed, walking like a trapped wolf, I staggered to my cell. Without replying to Philippe's greeting, I slipped under my too cold and too thin blanket. I stuffed my face in my pillow but didn't cry. But it took so much effort that my eyes were sweating.

14

ERUDITION

If you can't be them, beat them, as Watson Churchill, a politician from Western Europe, liked to say. I watched a documentary about him on the Documentary Channel between two police investigation shows. During one of the world wars, Churchill had turned out to be pretty useful at beating skinheads and German Nazis. Stalin did most of the heavy lifting, but the little bald guy skilfully played his cards right. The most important thing isn't to win the war but to be the one who benefits most from it. Churchill inspired me. Stalin too, in different ways. I hoped to use the strategies of the first to live in the opulence enjoyed by the second.

I slept on it and decided, fuck it, fuck everyone. I was going to kill three birds with one stone: free my boss, climb up the criminal hierarchy, and escape with my lover. I'd take advantage of Big Dick's helicopter escape to escape myself, on foot. It's less impressive but it could be just as effective. Yes, I would escape. Thin Lizzy warned you: tonight there's gonna be a jailbreak somewhere in this town.

You have to take chances when they come. Especially since I was being promised a job as a hit man on the outside: a hired assassin for the Italians is pretty high-end! I'd have a team to protect me and more money than I could burn through. And that was without even taking into account that Big Dick would be in my debt. Impressed by my sense of initiative, he'd be quick to pull some strings and get me into the top circles. Once I was safely out, with our escape pulled off, they'd ease off on the searches. I wouldn't be surprised if they gave me the responsibility of some big area of Montreal. Saint-Michel or Outremont, maybe. In any case, I'd need to work on my English, the official language of the metropolis. I was thinking big!

It was written in the stars, I was going to take my love hostage and then take her gently. I would wait for Big Dick to get through the three doors controlled by the boxes, be out in the yard, and flown away in a chopper, and then, with Edith in my arms, I'd leave too. My promised one wouldn't need to work anymore, especially not with the mentally ill types you find in prison.

She would stay by my side, obviously. She'd already told me that we'd still see each other even if I was transferred to a different prison. It would be even better when I get out. We'll live in a luxury pad in Laval, with a big chrome pickup, a boat, and the new identity that Cossa Notra will organize for me.

Even my mother would recognize me and come to live with us. I'd eliminate her dirty fat Greek, who isn't even my father, and everything would work out. I wouldn't have anything to do except give my wife a son and go to Sears for family photos. Let the good times roll once we were rolling in dough. Edith inspired me.

Yes indeed, our relationship of exceptional trust was strong enough for that. Even when I was free, despite being able to choose any woman I wanted, I would stay with her. I'd pay for a whore now and then, but it doesn't count if you pay for it. My soul would belong to her. I was tearing up. We'd build our paradise together, happy, with children that looked like us. Or better still, with pedigree dogs.

My plan was awesome; I could have kissed myself. I would have to obey my boss's orders but I'd earn as much as, if not more than, him. In the art of making the most of a situation, I was a fabulous artist. If anyone had loved me, they'd have been proud of me.

The passing days were as boring as fake boobs. I played the quiet soldier, trying to avoid attracting attention, staying chilled out and refining my plan. I read stacks of books, especially graphic novels. I have a soft spot for superheroes, they remind me of myself. I'd have liked a laser beam to melt Edith's heart, but she was maintaining the status quo. A passionate platonic relationship.

Our meetings were littered with ambiguous signals, but she never let down her guard. I had to do violence to myself to avoid revealing my plans to her, luring her with the promise of our future. Pretty soon she wouldn't have to act anymore or pretend to be professional. As the responsible man, I would free us both with my escape. But I had to keep the project secret to assure its success. It was hard. Secrets are like shameful illnesses: the challenge is keeping them to yourself. I was sealed off from the world, all alone in monastic silence. I bathed in the sweats of an endless summer, but I didn't let a single drop fall.

One day at a time. One week at a time. The prison routine: wheeling and dealing, jerking off, television. The heat wave was dragging on, getting everything bogged down in boredom. Until the nineteenth of August.

One of the only people who didn't know the score was scoring a whuppin' for himself. When I came out of my cell for breakfast, Colossus was huffing and puffing at Pedo and whacking him on the head with a newspaper. Tony was ignoring the whole thing with incredible fortitude, and he was even positioned in front of the observation box to block the view.

You know I'm first to get the paper, you jerk! You think it's yours, you think you have rights? I'm gonna shove it up your ass! Then you'll know what pain is, asshole!

What a prince! I found out more information while I was buttering my bread. Gilbert told me that Pedo was the first to touch the newspaper that morning. Colossus wanted news on the previous night's shooting in Old Montreal. His brother had been at one end of the gun—but it wasn't clear which end. In gangs, there's always weapons to spare, but never enough information. So Colossus had gone into Pedo's cell to get the paper, but the article he wanted had been torn out.

I don't get it, why didn't Pedo juft give him back the pave he'd ripped out?

Right then, Colossus was gripping Pedo's head and making him a lot of promises. And he intended to keep them. Gilbert continued, *That's the problem, he did give it back to him, but he'd torn it out for the other side of the page. It was a back-to-school ad, with lots of pretty photos of fresh kiddies.* He raised his eyebrows to underline the point.

Right, I get it!

The eyebrows went down. *So he gave him the page back, but it was all crumpled up and, uh, soiled.*

And boom! Colossus finished off his argument with a vigorous elbow blow to Pedo's nose. The nose burst open like a tap, bleeding like crazy, which earned him from that moment the nickname Pedo the Clown.

By the time Tony finally separated the two enemies, Paul,

the other guard on duty, had come running back from the showers to lend a hand. He was followed by two naked guys who didn't want to miss a thing. In a battle, it's the first blow that counts. Especially if there's only one.

Paul was yelling at Tony now, saying he should have called for him sooner or radioed for reinforcements from the next wing. Tony was saying that everything had kicked off too fast, but Paul wasn't buying it. Their bickering worried me. If the betrayal of our corrupt guard was revealed, my mission could be compromised. Those pigs seemed to suspect him already. It was hard having to trust other people—other people are never reliable.

Colossus's elbow had managed to settle the disagreement, he no longer had an argument with Pedo the Clown. But he refused to let himself be taken to isolation. While the guards were struggling to drag him down to the hole for a rest, I noticed that all the other guys in the wing were gathered around the toaster. They were cursing Pedo the Clown and cheering Colossus. It was a noisy scrum.

I took advantage of the chaos to execute the first step of my plan. Nimbly, stealthily, I rushed into Colossus's cell, ran over to the sink, picked up the object I desired, stuffed it back down my pants, and went back to the group, which was gradually dispersing, without anyone noticing me. Like a ninja. Or a poet.

Edith liked flowers, especially mine. I'd noticed that when I gave her my paper rose. Her face got all flustered, split between a questioning look and what I read as a grimace to hide her all-consuming passion. I was going to spoil her this time. In preparation for our follow-up meeting, I spent all morning making her a bouquet.

When I arrived at the office, I held it out to her and said

Ta-daaaa!

There was an emotional silence. *I don't know what to say.*

I like taking women's breath away. She held the seventeen paper flowers, filled with love, by their stems. Her insatiable virgin face was sending me a desperate message. We could no longer continue to keep our love secret.

We have to put our cards on the table now, I've talked to Antoine.

My doubtful look caused her to clarify. *With Tony.*

Right, the corrupt little piggy who's trying to play in my sandbox.

I can assure you, we absolutely do not have any emotional relationship.

Poor thing, she's worried I'll leave her, that I'm angry that Tony's sniffing around her.

I know. It'f not your fault.

She seemed even more beautiful. *I don't know what you're imagining, but it's really not what you think, our relationship is entirely professional.* She put the flowers down on the desk but stayed standing. *If you think we can't have a professional relationship, without expecting something else, they'll put a stop to these meetings. They'll find another officer to take your case on until you're released.*

No, it'f fine, don't worry. Wow, Edith was reacting strongly. Even if I was kinda jealous, I didn't want to end things just because of that. I reassured her. *I believe you. You juft have a profeffional relationfip.*

She laid it on even thicker. *Us! The two of us only have a professional relationship.*

I didn't get why she was going on about it so much. It worried me; if she needed to make such a big deal about it, then maybe there really was something between the two of them. Probably it had just been some flirtation before our trust relationship. She wouldn't dare cheat on me. *It'f fine, relacf, I get it!*

Okay, if we're all clear, let's get on with it.

I was expecting a first kiss on the lips for the flowers. But I understood that danger was all around. If someone came into the office, or was filming her without her knowledge, her career would be in jeopardy. My entire being was vibrating with the idea of telling her that we would be outside soon, that nothing would be impossible anymore, that our bodies would caress, feel, mingle, and intertwine with each other until we were satiated.

Are you listening to me?

Forry, I wav juft thinking of fomething important. Lost in my thoughts, I hadn't even noticed that she'd sat down.

The thing that worries me is that there are a lot of major things going on in your life right now. You're showering and eating with the big man. You do realize this will hurt your chances of early parole when the time comes?

Now I understood why she was so tense! *You think I might not get out affoon af I thought?* Don't worry, my sweet boo, we'll be together in a few days at most.

You have a long sentence to serve, a long sentence during which you're supposed to work on yourself rather than on "new relationships."

Right, I get it now. She's jealous of my friends, but I can't say a word about her little flirtation with Tony. To avoid pouring oil on the fire, I didn't push it further.

I am working on myfelf! I'm trying to ekfpreff my emoftionf… I let the last words slip out in a sugary voice, glancing meaningfully at her bouquet of roses.

Well, yes, but that doesn't mean your new friendships won't hurt you, both in the short term and the long term.

Her training as a guard dog in the justice system had brainwashed her so that she could no longer see the big truth. Whether in public or in private, crime's the only thing that pays.

I didn't worry too much about her naive illusions around

the whole concept of justice. When she saw me at the wheel of my big chrome pickup, my body covered with ink and bling, she'd understand that some values are more valuable than others.

At dinner, surrounded by the usual silence, I scarfed down my hash browns with ketchup. I was used to the funereal atmosphere at my table, but I envied the others. Philippe was playing cards with Gilbert the moonshiner, who cursed as he threw a match down onto the table. At ten dollars a match, the debts were spiralling fast.

Pedo the Clown's gang no longer had a leader since the episode with Colossus. Ever since Colossus had come back from the hole, Pedo had holed himself up. He no longer left his cell. This didn't stop his peers from mumbling in a brotherly fashion, wiping the spit from the corners of their mouths.

The black guys laughed as they mocked Xavier Dolan on the screen. The film director was posing in his usual chilled-out fashion, the victim of an interview by an overexcited little beauty at the red carpet. I couldn't figure out what the black guys thought was so funny. Life must be pretty great when you're young, rich, and famous like Xavier. He must fuck a lot of girls, get all the pussy he wants. All over the world. He probably films himself too, the fucker. With his gorgeous signorinas and fraüleins and kobietas and chiquitas and chicks, all around the world! I bet he has miles of film of crouching babes and hidden smokin'-hot mamas!

Denis was getting impatient. *Do you have the piece?*

I was so unused to him talking to me that I jumped. *No, I don't have the piece!* I was picking my teeth worriedly when he clarified.

The blade, do you have something to make a shiv?

With all the nicknames for people and objects there are in prison, you can sometimes lose the thread.

Oh, right, yef, I have fomething, don't worry.

Big Dick clicked his tongue and spat out a chunk of chicken bone. *We're not worried, you're the one who should be worried. This is the chance of a lifetime, kid, the only one you'll get!*

They left me with the crazies and Xavier Dolan, who was still going on about how original he was. I reckoned he was going to fuck the interviewer the second the cameras stopped rolling. Lucky bastard! When I turned around, I was smack in front of Louis-Honoré's face, which was twisted with hostility. You'd almost have thought he wanted to hurt me. He's a good actor. Ever since I'd found out that the whole thing was a front, I'd appreciated their acting work. Those guys were seriously talented. The guards were completely oblivious.

My doves were waiting for me, surrounded by half a dozen fucking pigeons on the make. I went up to them slowly and almost managed to kick one. But I also frightened my friends. *Don't worry, it'f juft the pigeonv I don't like. Rhoo hoo hooo. Come to Daddy. I knelt down by the fence. Pitipitipiti. Rhoo hoo hoo.* I had to wait almost five minutes, but they did come back. And for the first time, they both came to eat out of my hand. Sometimes the male, sometimes the female. I made a little hollow in my palms to force them to climb on my fingers and my arms. It tickled, I imagine it felt even nicer than a caress.

Everyone makes a big deal about human contact, but animals just do it without making a fuss.

15

INDULGENCE

With sweat dripping off me, I tried to catch my breath. I was afraid, but most of all I was disturbed. I had a solid erection in my right hand and was wiping my forehead with the left. I didn't have a hand spare to take my pulse, but it must have been galloping. I was coming around from an erotic nightmare. Under orders—and a leather whip—from Edith, my mother was straddling me as if I were a little animal ride in a mall. She was fucking me.

Mama wouldn't stop scratching my body and hissing obscenities. *Do you like that, my little kitty, tell me you like it!* But I was gagged. I couldn't yell at her to stop or tell her I liked it. And Edith was cackling away, stroking herself with the handle of the whip.

I could feel my mother's hot vagina sliding obstinately away on my penis. I was worried about getting her pregnant. You should always wear protection during incest. But no, it was too late, my mother was screwing me with great skill, and I was going to come inside her, fertilize her—and then I was saved by the wake-up bell. I groped for meaning in vain but couldn't even catch my breath.

I had to face up to the evidence. From a dream standpoint, I was a motherfucker.

It took me a good half-hour to get over it. Fucking your mother is fucking disgusting, even in a dream. Luckily I had a lot on my plate with the escape preparations. It helped me focus.

Sitting on the edge of my bed, I kept an eye out for Philippe or a guard coming in. I didn't have any reason to be afraid of Philippe, he was in the same gang as me, after all. Anyway, Big Dick had explained to me that everyone knew what they needed to know, and nobody else knew what I knew. I'd figured out that, as a member of the select inner circle of the top ranks of the wing, and employed as a Mafia hit man, I had secrets to keep. Including those of Operation Escape. Denis had forbidden me to use that name and ordered me to stop making names up, but I like naming operations. It makes me happy. So in my head I was getting ready for Operation Escape.

A noise made me sit bolt upright. It was just Tony, that loser, pretending to do a round of checks. I concentrated on making my weapon. I was rubbing my toothbrush on the cement floor, in a triangle of around four square inches where I'd scratched the paint off. Or I should say Colossus's toothbrush. Or really I should say Colossus's toothbrush handle, which was looking more and more like a knife, straight and nice and sharp.

Colossus hadn't mentioned the loss of this hygiene implement. He must have wanted to avoid a search. Maybe Big Dick had guessed what I'd done and had ordered him to keep his trap shut and let me work in peace. Anyway, when they showed him afterwards that it was his toothbrush that had been used in the spectacular double escape, I'd be long gone. And promoted above him in the hierarchy. The black guys stay at the bottom of the ladder in the Mafia. It's a Sicilian tradition.

After nearly an hour of artisanship, I had a plastic blade that could cut leather. It was a beautiful weapon, thank you, Colossus. I could have used my own toothbrush, sure. But just like James Bond, I wanted to be well armed *and* have clean teeth. Not forgetting, too, that Jocelyn had his eye on me, and I was already suspected of being implicated in the attack on Butterfly. I was a professional now; I had to cover my tracks.

I'd have to cover them even better once I was out of my cage. I'd have all the pigs and their dogs on my tail. Journalists too. But I'd like that part. Today, thanks to media attention, crime is finally getting its fair shake. It was well-deserved recognition. Gangsters are the last wild mustangs, the last rebels in this orderly world.

Any imbecile can write a novel, drag their ass around the four corners of the globe, or nail their ass to the seat until someone gives them a degree. But having enough balls in their heart to kill another human, well, that's not something just anyone can do.

The average citizen, ugly and illiterate, wouldn't even be able to name three Canadian presidents or four Indigenous nations. Yet he knows Ted Bundy, Charles Manson, and Karla Homolka. We're all fascinated by criminals, especially by murderers.

When you're a nothing, becoming less than nothing gives you a sense of worth. It's hard being an unknown in a world built on recognition. So all methods are good, even the bad ones. Never underestimate the power of negative reinforcement. And that makes for good news, a good editorial, high emotions among the population. Everyone's a winner.

On Thursday afternoon I gathered up my pile of books to renew them and consult the Sage. Paul escorted me. Paul was a big, dull, skinny guy who rarely spoke. He must have been thinking about digestion problems or marital frigidity. I told him I'd guessed what was on his mind. He retorted that my diagnosis wasn't worth shit and that his private life was absolutely none of my business.

He steered the conversation toward reading. He was a fan of Norwegian crime. Boooooring! He wouldn't drop it, he thought they had a unique style and original prose. I pointed out you always had to put up with the same atmosphere and the same riddles, and anyway, if he wanted stories about murderers all he needed to do was take a quick tour of the cells.

No, the thing I like about Scandi noir is how everything fits together. You don't have all the gratuitous violence of psychos who just kill for fun or to make a name for themselves, so it's a change from what I see all round me.

I felt my identity, my deepest values, attacked. *It'f the fame for uf, it'f juft that there'f no narrator to cook it all up and pop it in your mouth. I bet every fingle one of uf haf a ftory, and probably even a hiftory.* I was getting carried away and my voice was louder than our steps echoing in the corridor. All the inmates are overflowing with extenuating circumstances, but they don't all express themselves as well as I do. You can reproach us for being egocentric and shutting ourselves away, but tell me one single animal that doesn't want to be alone and roll up in a ball when it's injured to lick its wounds. We needed to be tamed.

You fould take an interest in the guyf you look after, that'f the real deal, more interefting than your Nordic ffhit. It'f too eafy to fay that it'f gratuitouf violenfe…

Don't take it personally, I'm just saying that the fictions are plotted out more elaborately, with an overarching structure guiding it—complicated plots that speak to me as a reader.

Well, Mr. Jerk, when you figure out what's going on right

under your eyes, and who's organizing what, you're going to be up to here in your very own Norwegian intrigue. When there's a chopper in your own yard, you're gonna care less about how green your neighbour's grass is.

But anyway, you ſould read the claſſicſ inſtead of thoſe dumb Fcandiwevian bookſ. The great Frenſh authorv are the baſiſ of modern thought. Boriſ Vian, Gilbert Camus, George Fand.

I know other important men wrote, but those were the ones that came to mind. I recommended them. *That'ſ what you ſhould read!*

Paul knocked on the library door. When the Sage let us in, the guard started up his mocking again. *So have you read all this?*

Yeſ, ſir, I've read ſo much that the library of Alexſandria would get loſt in my head.

He gave an admiring laugh, posted himself in the doorway, and let me find my friend.

The Sage was kind of down, his face greyer than lead. I was sad too, I was hoping he'd argue my side, against the Scandi scribblers. But the Sage wasn't in a party mood, he wasn't really in the mood for anything. It was official, he wasn't going to be released. In different circumstances I'd have been really happy about that. But I knew I'd be free myself before too long, forced to leave him alone with his books. I could only try to comfort him. *That'ſ a ſhame, the Fave, you deſerved it… You could have brought up your girlv, found a job, lived free… That'ſ a real ſhame!*

It bothered me, seeing him depressed like that. It's hard to know what to say to someone who's heard everything. This wasn't his first freefall. Knowing his daughters were growing up without him on the outside was too hard. He'd once told me he'd been taking antidepressants for eight years, and not recreationally. And he was falling once more. You have to be careful: depressions are like scowls: if the wind changes, you might get stuck like that.

I wanted to rub his back in a heterosexual and unambiguous

manner, just to be kind. But Paul cut me off. *No physical contact!*

That fucking Norwegian reader did everything by the book. I was going to have to do my work orally. It would do, I was pretty exceptional at therapy. I'd have made an excellent psychologist, social worker, or hairdresser. *Stop, the Fave, pleave don't cry…*

I could immediately tell he felt better. He held back his tears, stopped his lips from trembling, and lifted his head up like a man.

There you go, that'f better. It'f juft a delay. You can try again necft year.

He looked me up and down with a dignity so profound that he could have been diving with Cousteau and solemnly warned me, *There won't be a next time.*

He seemed very determined, which was a good thing. If he chose to do his time right up to the end of his sentence, that was his right. *That'f your right!*

The moment was too tense for me, since I was already too tense myself. The therapy could end now, it had been quick and effective and there was nothing else left to say.

Okay, now I need fome advife!

Paul had left his post to go and rummage around in the farthest shelf, the French novels section. Bravo! He'd refuse to admit it, but he was taking my advice. The shelf was bursting with the jewels of French literature, and especially Quebec literature. They even had one of Céline's novels there, if you can believe it.

Since the library consisted of just four shelves, I interrogated the Sage in a low voice. *I'm going to need a book about efcape tactics, camouflave, and foreft furvival.* I followed up with an obvious wink, but the Sage didn't pick up on it. He headed off to the illustrated-book section—the one that cruelly lacked a copy of the Karma Sutra. However, it did have a book of nude paintings. It was the most read book in the place. You have to remember that sculpture and painting were the pornographic mediums of antiquity. They are used once more for their original purpose in prisons.

The Sage, familiar with all the nooks and crannies of his domain, quickly put his hand on precisely what I wasn't looking for. A book about the great outdoors. *This is all I have. They're pretty selective about what they let in here.*

I agreed. *Fucking fenforfip!* Once more I was going to have to trust my instincts. I took the book, in case I had to hide away in a forest before I could get to my Mafia family in Montreal.

You need to prepare for every possibility. Once I was out of the prison walls, I could steal a car, but I'd be followed immediately. Or I could hide out in the woods, covering myself in mud like a modern-day Danny Crockett and travel under cover of wood and forest all the way to Montreal. It should take me a day or two from Donnacona if I walked fast.

I also borrowed books by J. K. Rowling and Robert Galbraith, as well as Camus's *The Stranger*, which I've never managed to finish. I didn't think I'd get any further this time, but I wanted to set a good example for Paul.

While my friend jotted down my borrowings with his trembling hand, nostalgia tied a knot in my throat. I realized that this would be my last visit. In a few days I would have made my escape, as part of the operation of the same name. I did think about including my librarian in my plan of escape, but it would be complicated, and Edith would resent me for jeopardizing our intimacy.

I promised myself I'd keep an eye out for books being published once I was established. If Vanier or Gérard Godin published a new poetry collection, I'd have one sent to the Sage inside. He'd know it was from me. You can spot the attentive people by their attention to the little things.

We'll fee each other foon!

No, we'll never see each other again…

He'd guessed my plans, clever guy. I gave him a final wink with my back turned toward Paul.

Goodbye…

Yef, my friend, fee you foon! I wanted to acknowledge his talent for reading between the lines but I wasn't going to let him advertise my plan. Depressed or not, learn some subtlety, dude! I quickly changed the subject and asked Paul, *Have you ever read* Doctor Vivago?

Of course he hadn't, because Zhivago wasn't a Norwegian author; I should have known. I chatted to him about French literature all the way back to my cell and then threw myself on my bed to explore my great-outdoors guidebook.

The great outdoors is stupid, almost as stupid as those jerks who like it. It's all about the equipment. You need such-and-such kind of boots, you should get this type of tent, the best thing is to get in touch with some expert on the national park where you want to go to enjoy nature, and blah blah blah. There was nothing about the wilderness outdoors if you were escaping, and nothing about edible plants just in case you forgot to make yourself a nice little lunch before you set off in your nice little high-end truck dressed in your fancy Gore-Tex outfit to take selfies at the top of a nice little mountain. If I had to hide out in a forest, eating bark, I'd need to know, at a minimum, which trees were poisonous. In a moment of foresight, I told myself I wouldn't just collect food for the birds now, I might need some myself too.

Disappointed, I closed the book. Sports literature always has that effect on me. Since Philippe wasn't there, I slid my hand under my mattress. The shank was still there, wedged against the cement bed base. A well-sharpened weapon is reliable, unlike sports literature. Read the newspapers, it's well documented.

Stress is stressful. I was getting excited and it was stressing out the people around me. I couldn't talk to my brothers in arms during the meal, and the black guys were playing their parts so well that they systematically ignored me. Philippe and Gilbert were getting involved in a poker game with a twenty-buck buy-in. All I had were the crazies.

I went to interrupt them watching an episode of *The Young and the Restless*, a series beloved by people with pharmaceutically induced holes in their heads. I guess they can relate to the bubbling of intrigues and emotional liaisons... Just kidding! What they like are the grooming strategies, and the visiting grandchildren, always nicely dressed.

Pedo the Clown, who was gradually coming back out of his cell, grumbled when I sat down in front of him. I teased him about his hunchback posture, his smell, his crooked teeth, and what I was planning to do to his mother. He didn't react. I wanted to interact with somebody so I kept pushing it. All he did was get up with a groan and head back to his cell.

I knew Beanpole and the other newbies less well, so I suggested a game of cards. mathieu said he didn't mind. *I don't mind...* The affirmative catchphrase of personalityless people everywhere. I convinced him, social organizer that I am, to get his ass out of his chair, and I extended the invitation to the whole room. Melon sniggered and headed over to my table.

He was continuing to play the idiot, unaware that his secret had been exposed, that I'd recognized his voice. Had Big Dick himself chosen him to move into our wing? Did he have a part to play in the boss's escape? Life is a field of questions where doubt grows.

I watched him struggle to fit his enormous thighs under the table. I didn't dare criticize Big Dick, but personally I wouldn't be able to trust someone who was obese. I don't feel comfortable around them. Just looking at them makes me feel guilty of a moral crime. Obesity is a socially acceptable form of self-harm. People like that should hide themselves away, it's unhealthy for everyone.

Considering the setting and the three of us around the table, I suggested an easy game: Asshole. It was straightforward, it could last for hours, and my chances of winning were good. I dealt the cards, slipped myself a pair of twos and set out to humiliate them. But I hadn't counted on Melon's deceit. He refused to react to my insults or to my accusations of cheating, he stubbornly insisted on staying President, he attacked me to help mathieu, and kept me in the unpleasant position of asshole the whole time. His smirking was getting on my nerves. I'd had enough of getting finessed. I stood up with dignity and let fly with my rage. *Go fuck yourfelf!*

If Fat Melon laughs at me, I can deal, I'm used to it. If the black guys slap their thighs and chuckle at me, I can't do anything about it. But when pathetic little mathieu thinks he can join in, that's just too much. I took advantage of the fact that he was still sitting down to raise my knee as high as I could and then I kicked him right in the spine. The shock alone could have shattered his bone marrow. That might have been an excellent result.

That sly mathieu turned out to be pretty socially awkward. He pretended to be all shy and introverted but then revealed he was a black belt in the art of counter-attack. I'd barely had time to thump him in the back when he leaped up and confidently launched himself at me. It took me by surprise. I was doing some crazy kick-boxing moves and throwing punches in all directions, without ever managing to hit my target. Galvanized by the encouragement of the entire wing, he was enjoying taking it out on my face. Under the rain—the storm—of blows, I fell back over a table and lay there, exposed. Belligerently he took advantage to brutalize my ribs and my balls with his rock-hard knuckles. It was like he was in a trance, the way he was attacking me.

I longed for my mother.

The most dangerous men are the ones with nothing to lose, because they have everything to win. mathieu was making his reputation with his punches to my face. Criminals are opportunists, and inmates are professional criminals. They were cheering my assailant on and calling for sacrificial murder. They were glorifying him. Unused to getting all this attention, mathieu was getting in some awesome shots despite his breathlessness. He was catching on to the fact that he'd gained some respect. From now on he'd be entitled to a capital letter at the beginning of his name. Mathieu was hitting me out of sheer joy.

Paul and Mireille stopped him mid-punch, to the boos of the other inmates. I stood up with difficulty, pointing out to everyone that I hadn't fallen. *Okay, he furprived me, but I didn't hit the ground, I didn't fall down!*

The guys were still cheering and applauding their new champion. I wiped my bloody lip and grabbed hold of the table, trying to steady my breathing. And my shaky body. I was beat and injured but still standing; like Gloria Gaynor, I will survive.

Although I was desperate to go and hide in my cell, I stayed as straight as a reed, rooted to the floor. The bastard had used the element of surprise, okay, but my honour was intact. I hadn't fallen to the ground. And standing upright in the common area, I reminded them of this. And I wasn't bleeding that much.

You idiot, you could have wrecked everything.

It was unusual for Denis to talk to me before dessert. Dinner was turning out to be livelier than usual.

I'm not going to fcrew anything up.

The shepherd's pie tasted of yesterday's fricassee.

If we hadn't covered for you and said it was the new guy who started it, you'd be the one in the hole. And who knows how long you'd have been there. Everything's all set to start in four days, for fuck's sake, this is no time for pissing around!

Denis was really telling me off. Which was nice. You only tell people off if you like them.

So keep quiet until the last minute, no more messing around, we need you. Even Big Dick was worried.

Don't worry, guyv, I'll be difcreet. The dried blood in my sinuses and my swollen lips were stopping me from fully enjoying the meal. *I'm not going to eat my pudding, do you want my pudding, Denif? Big Dick?*

Apparently none of my colleagues had a sweet tooth.

Alone at our table, I sat patiently and let my digestion do its thing. I'd just been worming things out of Paul. He was still trying to teach me about literature, crushing my balls with his thing about signifier and signified. I just wanted to signify to him that he was insignificant. But I held back; I'm less impulsive than the psychiatrists claim.

I let him babble on about semantics before asking him about my love. She had no known partner and no crush, not even Tony. The question surprised him. No, he didn't know whether she'd kept my paper roses. Yes, she was very professional. Yes, this week she was working the evening shift. He wouldn't tell me anything else, and anyway, I shouldn't be asking questions about the correctional officers. My dear Paul, I'm not interrogating you about a correctional officer but about my love. There's a subtle difference!

I sat and waited for her, all alone with my empty tray. In the end I gave in and ate the pudding. I was licking out the bowl when I heard the metallic clang of the massive steel door. This noise was followed by the electronic opening mechanism and the creaking of the hinges. The heavy door of the wing took forever to open partway, before letting through my queen in the glow of garish neon.

How could I have doubted her beauty? There is no worse blind man than one who pokes his own eyes out. In my hatred of the guards, I'd once put her in the same category as Fat Mireille. And here she was, exhausted but radiant. And upset too; she headed right for me with her hand held out. I kept my head high, showing off my injuries, proud as a kid getting his cast signed in the schoolyard. Women like injured men. It turns on their internal nurse. They all have an internal nurse; it comes with the uterus.

She put her hand on my forehead, or rather on the bump hiding my forehead. Gently. She looked at my split lip and then my eyebrow.

My ribs hurt too. I didn't dare tell her about my balls—she might start worrying about our future.

But what happened?

I sighed a bit to arouse her. *I got attacked, totally blindsided. I didn't do anything.*

Compassion and desire were competing in her doe eyes. *So why did it happen?*

I'd prefer it if we could talk in private, in the office.

Jocelyn showed up next, but he was less tender than Edith. My lady love explained the situation to him, hoping for a chance to spend time with me. She asked him to keep his eye on the gang of crazies. He agreed, knowing full well that after dinner the vast majority of them would be knocked out by meds, whether prescribed or not. Not forgetting the fact that the black guys had managed to smuggle in a long cylinder of hashish via Louis-Honoré's sister. Two shipments actually: those Montreal North girls are very open. Open-minded, I mean, obviously.

Our visiting room had more holes than a pair of fishnets. On the outside, those guys are all about the coke and cognac. Inside it's all hash and Klonopin. That shows an incredible ability to adapt.

Limping slightly, I followed my love to the office. I realized that my physical injuries were less painful than my frustrated desires. I'd had enough of this back-and-forth, push-me-pull-you nonsense, without ever actually getting any. And that was on top of all the worry and chaos of the last few months. This game of impossible love, all the waiting, was burning up my soul. She loved me, all the signs had shown up one after another. From our "relationship of trust" to her wearing her hair loose, via physical contact. And just a minute earlier she'd been stroking my head. Hypnotized by her enormous pelvis, which could have birthed an entire Amish colony, I promised myself I'd kiss her when I went into the office.

As I walked in, I kissed her. I did warn you. She shut the door behind us, I pressed her up against the wall, my hands on her hips. She squeaked in surprise but let me do it, girls are like that. My lips were palpitating with desire. I glued them on hers, stuck my tongue in and gave it a passionate wriggle. She didn't squeak again, but she didn't let me do it. I didn't even have enough time to get my tongue in her cheek before she caressed my testicles with her knee, hard. *Hmmpf.* Twice.

Hmmmmmmmpf.

The genital chakra is a man's centre. It's also the place where he hinges. I folded immediately, grabbing her shoulders. I wound up with my face in her neck. In spite of the agonizing pain, I took a second to breathe in. Sweet women's perfume. Luxury fragrance, probably some high-end brand like J-Lo or Paris Hilton. Before I'd had a chance to make a clever remark about Patrick Süskind's work, she pushed me with both hands against the desk and screamed. I spread out on the files strewn all over the desk.

I got up immediately. She had blood on her lips; probably mine. It must have been the taste of blood that surprised her. It wasn't very sensitive of me to kiss her with all my injuries. Feeling confused, I was going to apologize for jumping the gun when Jocelyn burst angrily into the room.

The door smashed into the wall, almost hitting my love. He must have noticed the blood on her face and not been smart enough to figure out that it was mine. The idiot thought I'd hit her, assaulted her, or something equally bad, so he jumped on me, flattening me like a pancake on the desk. I tried to explain, to make him understand that it wasn't what he thought, but he pressed my face into the desk, spreading my blood over the strewn files.

I don't often get a chance to use the word *strewn*, so I suppose that's a silver lining.

Poor Edith was powerless and overtaken by events. She was still backed up against the wall, paralyzed, while Jocelyn yanked me upright, handcuffs on my wrists, arms behind my back. Then backup arrived. Paul started waving his pepper spray around, trying to season me. Jocelyn, that pathetic little cock, sent him away, assuring him that he had both me and the situation under control. He was going to put me in the hole.

But I didn't do anything!

As he dragged me out of the office, Jocelyn yelled at my fellow inmates to shut their mouths. They were all there, shouting and clapping. I'd given them a whole day of entertainment. No one was missing, except for Pedo the Clown, who was succumbing to anxiety in his cell. They were all cheering Jocelyn's catch, except for Big Dick and Denis, who had faces like thunder on a stormy night. Denis even made a pretty unbrotherly gesture, moving his thumb across his neck, slowly, from one ear to the other.

The whole time we were going along the corridor to the hole, I was trying to figure out the meaning of what I'd just seen. He couldn't be threatening me with death, right? I was a brother in arms, a Mafia hit man, a crucial cog in the wing boss's escape plan. But here I was heading toward the hole and probably wrecking everything. This time I could admit it.

I didn't want to make a big deal out of it nor put my foot in it. Maybe Denis was just telling me that I was in deep shit, right up to my neck. I know how to swim though, so maybe I could still get out of it. I was trying to convince myself, but my hopes were thinner than an anorexic cocaine addict.

How long I am going to be in the hole?

Shut up and keep walking! Jocelyn must not have had regular massages, he was getting stressed.

It'f important, how long am I going to be there?

Until you get transferred somewhere else. There's no forgiveness if you assault a guard.

My world was crumbling around me. Amid all the wreckage of my future, I was worried about my love.

Edith must have been in despair. Look at the mess she'd got us into!

16

CONCENTRATION

It's hard to kill time when patience is your only weapon. For three whole days I did yoga. That's a type of Indian stretching. The basic idea is to lengthen your limbs in any direction while maintaining an expression of deep focus. It's healing. My body was a total pain show and it looked like a rainbow, if you'll pardon the poetic licence. Mauve and yellow at the edges, black at the eye socket, and brown and orange at the groin.

I checked out the graffiti in between two cold meals. Nothing new. After I'd read them twenty times, I knew them all by heart.

When there's nothing left to read
It's time to write, take heed.

That was by Balzac, an author.

With a broken fingernail, I scratched Edith's initials under mine. I did them all as stylized letters, really putting my heart into it. It was incredible gothic calligraphy, as beautiful as a tattoo. Even in this grey paint, our love would stand the test of time. I was just finishing up the heart, framing the whole thing, when they came to take me out of the hole. My lawyer wanted to talk to me. His little legal-expert face was as ugly as the beauty of the news he was bringing me.

I was soaring: I was going to be returned to my wing. All the prisons were over capacity and nobody wanted to accept another crazy. And since I was already in a protected wing, it was administratively impossible to move me internally.

Fuckin lit!

The lawyer wasn't quite so enthusiastic. I was so eager to get back to my gang and my love that I got carried away. *Fuckin lit even if you don't give a shit.* I wasn't going to let a lawyer kill my joy.

You must have the luck of a cuck, but the agent you assaulted isn't going to press criminal charges.

Well duh, dumb-ass, I didn't assault her, she's my wife. *And why are you going on about cucks? She didn't say I was a cuckold, did she?*

The lawyer sank back in his chair. His smile evaporated under the sun of my anger.

Calm down, it's just an expression. You're not literally a cuckold, I swear, at least not to my knowledge…

I hate it when people use these archaic regional expressions to make themselves look clever.

Your expression's stupid. Cuck yourself!

Paul took me back to our wing. He stayed silent the whole way. He was sulking with me. Jealous of my idyll with Edith, no doubt. The guards must have gossiped about our kiss. And about Jocelyn, playing the cowboy and getting involved in things that didn't concern him. How they must have gossiped about my case. I was no longer a crazy like the others now. I was half of a couple that included one of their colleagues, sitting at the table with the king of the wing, I was becoming someone important. But it was still a shame. I liked Paul, even if he did read a load of crap.

Tony welcomed me back with a complicit and threatening smile. A few guys sitting around the TV said hi, some calling me Don Juan and others calling me Sicko. I liked the nicknames. Soon I'd have to choose an official one for the media. What with the escape and the career I had lined up, I'd be all over the headlines. I hoped they'd use a photo that made me look good. Positive self-representation is a primordial desire. As Bill Cosby showed us, the important thing about reputations is having a good one.

I thought I'd be taken back to my cell, where I could read quietly while waiting for Denis, Big Dick, or Godot, if it came to that! We had to organize a summit to sort everything out and relaunch Operation Escape. But instead Paul took me to the office. Was this another nice surprise? My heart was thumping away, I was going to see Edith again. What a naughty girl, she'd schemed so that we could meet up as soon as I was let out of the hole. I was very touched.

Jocelyn was waiting for me, his hands flat on the desk, which was empty this time, with absolutely nothing strewn across it. I was expecting to find my wife, but instead I found myself with this puffed-up superhero wannabe. The human adventure is just one long string of failures and disappointments shot through with a few hopeful moments that give us the strength to continue our suffering… I was philosophizing as I pulled out a chair.

You can probably guess I'm not very happy to see you back here.

I jumped at his throat and ripped open his jugular with my teeth…in a parallel reality, some quantum universe.

Well, I hope you realive I'm not too ecfited about feeing your fafe either!

I mentally X'd that bastard out. Sooner or later I'd deal with his case. As soon as I get the chance, I'm going to get my revenge list tattooed on my arms, my thighs too if I need more space. Jocelyn will be right at the top in big letters.

I have no choice about you coming back to the wing, at least for now. But it won't last. Meanwhile, let's get one thing clear: we won't tolerate a single wrong move from you. And above all, most importantly, while Edith is waiting to move to a different section, you will not approach her and you will not speak a word to her.

Eureka! I understood. All of a sudden everything fell into place.

It wasn't Tony who was the threat, it was that bastard Jocelyn. He was the little fucker who was crushing on my Edith. I should have figured it out sooner, should have understood why he was so keen to protect her, why he gave her shifts at the same time as his, why he hurled himself at me that time Edith let me know that I'd moved too fast. And above all, it explained why he wanted to transfer me and transfer her as well, so he could well and truly stop me from seeing my beloved.

If I see you go near her, talk to her, or even think about her, I swear I'll make you regret it.

The mangy three-legged son of a bitch! He would pay for this, pay for the rest of his life.

I left the office fuming and went straight to take refuge in my cell and, without even paying any attention to whether Philippe was there or not, I slipped my hand under my mattress and pulled out my blade.

Whoa, man, what are you doing with that?

I immediately hid it inside my underwear, stood up, and took on the immigrant. *You know very well what I'm going to do with it! We're in the fame boat, aren't we?*

Fear suited him. *Yeah, man, sure, whatever you say.*

I calmed down a little. *I'm going to do what I have to do with thif… Defend myfelf and my honour.*

Okay, man, do what you gotta do, I gotta go!

He bolted, leaving me alone in our crib. Perfect. I wanted to think about the meaning of life and death of others.

I didn't have time to get into a deep trance. Denis appeared at the door.

Hey, champ…

Hi! I didn't like his attitude. We were colleagues, he didn't have to put on the condescending airs of a convenience-store manager.

Follow me!

Pleave.

What?

Follow me pleave, don't give me orderv.

Denis jumped on me, grabbed me by the throat, and pinned me to the ground, bashing my head into the cement floor. I shoved my hand in my underwear, grabbed my blade and then, through my clothes, I stabbed him right in the gut. Again and again and again! His blood was spurting out, his body was emptying. He was screaming blue murder, his eyes begging for mercy. *Nooooo, I'm dying!*

This was all in my head, but it's what I should really have done, if only I'd known.

Denis was still pressing me into the ground and strangling me. *You fucking imbecile, I can give you all the orders I like! You almost wrecked a plan that took months to put together. We thought we could rely on you but you're just another crazy fucker!*

I tried to argue. *Hhhhaaiirrrghh…* but it was futile.

So yes, you will follow me and yes, you will follow orders!

Denis was cranky, a guy who liked to make storms in teacups. I wouldn't go as far as labelling him violent, but he was definitely trigger-happy. After all, I'd have followed him without making a fuss if he'd just asked politely.

Jocelyn showed up while Denis was still sitting on top of me.

Am I disturbing a private moment here, gentlemen?

I was busy catching my breath, so I let Denis handle the situation.

No, my buddy fell over, I was just helping him get up.

Jocelyn frowned. *You should be more careful when you choose your friends, Denis.*

He wasn't helping his case.

Yes, I agree.

I could have said a lot of things to both of them, but my silent scorn had to do.

While we were heading over to Big Dick's cell, Melon blocked our path. Denis shoulder-checked him. It's an old convict's trick for passing stock, letters, or weapons. I turned back just in time to spot Melon's nod to Colossus, who was at the far end of the common area. Something big was brewing, maybe even bigger than what I was brewing myself. Adrenaline flooded my spine via the raw-nerve highway.

Big Dick was perched on the edge of his bed, as though we were shooting a second take of our first meeting. I knew the protocol and sat down opposite him while Denis kept guard at the door. The boss didn't welcome or greet me but just sat there holding eye contact. But I was still proud and wasn't going to lower my eyes first. Thwack! He swung his fist at my face.

For fuck's sake, seriously, are you going to stop? Thwack again. No, shut it, you little jerk, I'm gonna hit you until you shut up for good and then you're gonna listen!

So obviously I pulled out my shank and rammed it through his eye and right into his brain…in my dreams. In real life, it's not exactly socially acceptable to kill a boss. Sure, it happens all the time, but it has to be a different boss, a former boss, or an aspiring boss who orders a sitting boss to be murdered. This wasn't the case here. So I did nothing except bleed from the nose and listen.

I am liʃtening! I accidentally sprayed a few drops of blood on him.

You're not listening, you can barely hear me! If you were listening, we wouldn't be in this mess right now.

He was right about it being messy.

I am liʃtening! I ʃwear!

Everything's going ahead tomorrow, just like we planned… With Edith, just like we planned. He was silent for a long time, waiting for a reaction from me. I put on my best impassive cold-fish face.

There's no problem with Edith?

I dabbled in my role like Pacino on set. *No problem, it'ʃ nothing, it waʃ all juʃt a big miʃunderʃtanding.*

He swallowed it. *Okay, great, we'll create a diversion in front of the box, Tony will stay to the side. We'll take care of it. All you have to do is take Edith into the office, shut yourself up in there with her, and wait for the police to call you to negotiate. Look, everything you have to ask them is on this piece of paper. Say nothing more, nothing less, just read these sentences, got it?*

My reply would soothe him. *That'ʃ too eaʃy!* I clicked my fingers to demonstrate.

No, no, seriously, it's not going to be easy, especially for you. But we have a plan B. Don't blow your chance… Silence…

I'm betting on my victory… Silence… *Iʃ that all?…* Starting to feel uncomfortable…

Go away!

Big Dick hadn't patted me on the shoulder or clasped my hand, he was too nervous. I was getting nervous too, with his whole plan B thing. Didn't he trust me anymore? Were there other crazies involved? And if his plan B affected my plan A, did I need to come up with a plan C? Everything seemed to point to yes.

On my way back, I passed Colossus, who bashed into me rudely even though he didn't have anything to give me.

Hey, asshole! You're going to be left without any protection soon, huh? Watch your ass!

On the level of strategies for diverting guards, it was well played. Except there were no guards around.

When I reached my cell, I came face to face with Mathieu. I raised my hands reflexively. My noble defensive instincts amused Philippe and his new buddy. He who laughs loudest dies last.

They were checking out tattoo designs. I was about to warn him that Japanese warriors were not a house specialty when Mathieu spoke up. He'd become more confident and been promoted since our fight; beating up another guy is still the best rite of passage for becoming a man.

Seems like they're giving you another chance?

I played it cool. *I don't need another ffhhanfe, I have talent.* My arms crossed over my chest underlined my confidence.

Haha, that's right, don't mess up your shot, you fag!

And whoosh. I didn't do anything to him then, but I gave him a VIP position on my revenge list, in the "multiple tortures" section. As Mao-Tseo said: sit down by the riverside and wait for the chance to drown your enemies.

I didn't know what to do with myself in my own cell. I shrank into the corner of my bed to read. It was reassuring to know I could always take refuge in literature. Every social reject loves a good book. But now even this last defence was collapsing, since Jocelyn came in and confiscated all my printed material with a smile on his face. I kicked up a fuss, threatened to take it to the highest authority. *I have the right to read bookf in my fell, my lawyer negofiated it! I'm going to complain to the manavement!*

Stop whining, you'll get your books back later. For now, we have to get them all back to the library. We have to do an inventory since the guy killed himself.

I froze in disbelief. *What? Whiff guy killed himfelf?*

The guillotine of the answer fell on the neck of my question. *That guy Sage. He hanged himself.*

He must have read too much Camus. Or Victor-Lévy Beaulieu, who's just as depressing. Existential questions aren't for everyone. My friend the Sage was no longer. It was a big loss for me, a giant loss for mankind. As the saying goes, a man of letters leaving us is a library burning with an old man inside.

The Sage had omitted to mention that he was a tragedy fan. The fall was brutal. I hadn't seen it coming, but then you can never see it coming. The truly suicidal never give any signs. It just happens like that, without warning, overnight. It's destiny.

I was disoriented before, but now I was completely rattled. I was taking my friend's death harder than I wanted to admit. It felt as though he had dug his grave in my very guts. There was an enormous internal void inside me. I felt dirty and wounded, and I had man ache. If I hadn't gone to take a shower, I'd have ended up crying.

It was my last dinner in prison. I was going to make a move the next day, at the first opportunity. I had no appetite. It was better that way. It meant I could suck the chunks of stewing beef and stash them in my underwear. Along with some bread, little cups of butter, and some salt packets. For my escape.

Fucking hell, you wanna tell me what you're playing at?

Despite my subtlety and stealth, Denis had picked up on

what I was doing. Telling him about my plan to escape after Big Dick got out was out of the question.

Nothing, I'm not doing anything, I juft get hungry at night.

There was an exasperated silence.

Well, if you hide your dinner in your pants, it's not that surprising you get hungry at night. He punctuated this observation with a long sigh of frustration, and then Big Dick started fretting about my mental state.

He has to be the worst crazy to ever come through this wing, and he's the one who's gonna get me out of here? Denis, remind me why the fuck this was a good idea?

They were exaggerating. Their bad faith was more noticeable than buttocks in a pair of leggings.

I stayed calm, guessing that their strategy was to talk theatrically about their loss of confidence in me to ensure my complete focus.

He did ice Butterfly though.

Big Dick corrected him: *Nearly iced Butterfly!*

We all turned mute as Paul moved between the tables.

Yes, technically…

Technically fffmechnically, I'll do what I have to do. There'v no need to worry, Big Dick. Pack your fuitcafe and fet your mind at eave.

And I finished the Last Supper, our last meal, slurping down my Jell-O. (Orange, the best flavour.)

I had my blade in my underwear, and the other inmates were rubbing up against me. That sounds very homosexual, but you have to take it literally: I was armed and caught up in the scramble to get out into the yard. It was always the same at outside time, all the guys wanted to be the first one through the doors. As if they personally were snatching the extra second they gained outdoors from the hands of freedom herself. The second they crossed the threshold, the excitement disappeared, everyone fell back into their usual habits, their slow, heavy footsteps, to take up their regular spot in the yard, day after day.

My doves were already waiting for me in my corner, cooing away. The pigeons knew they'd get nothing from me and flew off when I showed up. I rolled the bread I'd saved into a few balls in the palm of my hand. Hunched over, I encouraged my proteges to come and eat. They took turns feasting, jumping from one hand to the other.

There is no answer to the great existential questions other than patience. Everything happens when you need it. You just need to be alert, read the signs and seize your opportunities. Scientists who specialize in chakras and angel energy will tell you the same thing. Good things come.

After all those months of taming, the male climbed onto my left wrist and the female onto my right. A dove was perched on each of my arms and pecking each of my hands. At last. And then: sshhhtriiiikkk. I squeezed my fists as hard as I could.

Aaaaaargh! I roared with contentment. They were mine!

The female jabbed her beak into my palm and beat her wings, imprisoned in my right fist. Her male, more tightly in my grasp, let out a coarse wheeze as I splintered his ribs, and his little black eyes popped out right to the ends of his optic nerves. *Rhaaaaa!*

I caught my breath, tightened my grip and yelled louder: *RHAAARGH!* I felt the male's body mould itself to my fist, his bones snapping and piercing his organs under the pressure. The female was shaking her butt like crazy, feathers were twirling around in the yard, blood was flowing down my flailing arm as she spasmed her last breaths. And then it was over. Her life had slipped away.

I dropped the corpses at my feet, wiped the sweat off my

forehead, and looked up. All the inmates, and the guards too, were staring at me in silence. Jaws had dropped. Beanpole was crying. The silence lasted a long time, right up to the moment when Melon fell to his knees and started throwing up.

17

SPONTANEITY

I slept badly, filled with a sensation of deep emptiness. Insomnia in prison is a stupid waste of time. It's like mixing nonbusiness with displeasure. My thoughts were scattered to the four points of the compass. I was suffering from my friend's death. The absence of Edith in my arms was weighing on me. I was already missing my doves, but I couldn't have left them here without me. And in spite of my concrete plan, I was afraid something would go wrong, some freak occurrence in the hostage-taking and the escapes.

I tossed and turned for hours. Every time sleep almost carried me off, a sudden fear whipped me into wakefulness. And Philippe, who wasn't asleep either, was moving just as much. He was getting on my nerves!

I'm trying to fleep, I have a big day tomorrow. Juft go to fleep, will you?

In a hesitant voice, he murmured, *Forget it, dude, I can't even close my eyes if you're not asleep.*

Paul did the morning head count, just before the shift change. Usually, just the noise of the doors being opened was enough to wake me up. That morning, the guard had to bang on the steel. Bang bang!

Get up! No sleeping in! Especially you, you need to come and sign the note in your file about yesterday's little performance.

Still in a fog, I couldn't work out what show he was talking about. The doves incident popped into my mind. *I wasn't putting on a performance, I wav juft trying to deal with my ftreff.*

I totally get that it was shocking for people who've been conditioned to eat dead animals but who never kill them themselves. People underestimate the feeling of well-being you get from killing something. Humans, obviously, but especially animals. It's more accessible and there are fewer consequences. And it's similar. A dying human is always closer to the beasts than to the angels.

The guards weren't the only ones bothered by my executions. The entire wing was giving me the death stare as if I were Hannibal himself. If they were trembling over two little doves, what were they going to think in a few hours when I was accused of aggravated murder? People shrank away from me as I passed, giving me free access to the much-coveted toaster. What hypocrites!

I was philosophizing to myself, filtering my thoughts through the cynical approach prism developed by Seneca. Killing animals is therapeutic. We shouldn't just stop at eating them, we should all kill them ourselves. That way we'd take on their suffering. The Americans can't even kill their convicts without any mistakes, so do we really think that the hundreds—thousands, even—of animals each person consumes per year don't undergo torture at the abattoir? Ha! We ought to have light bulbs attached to our foreheads so we can see when we're hiding our heads up our asses.

As I was buttering my toast, I noticed Tony arriving, taking over from Fat Mireille. Edith would be replacing Paul any minute now. All I had to do was wait for a chance to meet her in the office to set off Operation Escapio. It sounds more Italian that way. The best part about being the only person who knows the name of your operations is being able to rename them whenever you feel like it.

Sitting alone at the table, I was whistling a bit of "Wind of Change" by Metallica. What with having toast crumbs on my tongue and being a tooth and a half short, it was a bit of a challenge: *Fffft ffft ffft ft ffft ffffiit!* I felt like I was graduating, or at least I imagine that's what it's like—I've never graduated anything. I was almost expecting someone to give me a yearbook. Short of making a scrapbook of miscellaneous news articles, I couldn't expect a collection of memories of my fellow inmates. I myself would soon be an inmate no longer.

For the final time, I breathed in the prison morning smell of burned bread mixed with the heat-wave sweat. I looked round at the old beige walls, the crazies' broken jaws, the precious television. I gazed for a long time through the barred windows at the yard where I used to go outside for an hour every day to take care of my doves. Then I cast my eyes down to my hands, these hands that were about to commit another crime, any minute now.

Denis slipped in next to me, excited, and anxious for reassurance.

Do you have everything you need? Do you have the paper? Do you have a weapon?

I just answered with a single yes for all the questions.

Good, perfect, they don't suspect a thing. I'm going to stay with you, make sure you don't do anything stupid! As soon as you're in the office, we're going to call the Italians to say the helicopter can take off. This is the real fucking deal, don't fuck it up. I was calm, confident, zen. Boy oh boy, was I relaxed, as Pedo might have said.

There was nothing to keep me here any longer. Everything was waiting for me outside: my career, my love life, my freedom. Big Dick's helicopter trip was just one little piece of my plan. And I was going to see it through.

Everything'v going to be juft fine, Denif.

I gave him a little pat on the hand and he immediately pulled his away, afraid that someone might spot us.

And look who was here, with all the noise of the doors opening, shining in the morning light, burning in my wolf heart. Her uniform suited her so badly. I was desperate to see her naked, to have her all to myself. She avoided my eyes and concentrated as Paul and Mireille brought her up to speed on things before the shift change.

Tony was already stationed at the far side of the communal area, strategic and completely useless. Big Dick must have given him his orders. From there he enjoyed an excellent view of the whole place: you'd have sworn he was doing his job, but he was mainly just keeping away from the office door.

Just be ready to go, I think it's going to happen. As soon as she's alone, you jump her and then force her into the office!

Denis was exhilarated, more excited than a virgin in a whorehouse.

Get ready, get ready...

And then big Melon came and squeezed in next to us. Without even bothering to slide his thighs into the gap meant for that purpose, he flopped into the seat, his loose blubber spread out on the table. He was blocking our view.

Denis went so stiff I thought he was going to explode. He channelled all his power into a whispered shout: *Fuck off, you fat fuck!*

Melon squinted at us, smirking.

Get the fuck out of here!

I deduced that Melon wasn't in on the plan.

Fuck. Off. Now!

He didn't move and wouldn't move. It was all pretty tense. I shoved my hand in my pants to grab my shank.

Denis stood up and grabbed me by the elbow. He wanted to reposition us, but I resisted, standing up to Melon.

I know you're juft pretending, I heard you talking to Coloffuf, what'f your problem?

Suddenly interested, Denis made sure that Edith was still with the group and sat back down. *Does this asshole talk?*

He knew how to talk and how to sweat, I was going to demonstrate.

We'll fee who'v laughing now, Mr. Comedian. I stood up. Melon followed me with his gaze and squinted at the ceiling with the other. I sat down beside him, opposite Denis. By pushing up against his flabby body, I was able to grab my blade with my right hand. I unceremoniously pressed it into the flesh of his ribs. *Talk, you baftard, we're liffening. Who'v your boff?*

Denis was hopping up and down on his chair. *Don't do anything stupid, for fuck's sake, we don't want to attract any attention!*

I needed to be clear in my own mind about it. I could feel that Melon's skin was about to split; my weapon was on the point of piercing it. I leaned in closer and increased the pressure.

Okay, okay, I'll talk, get that off me!

There was a floating sensation, like a corpse rising to the surface of a swamp. I had my proof; silence was still the best defence.

I was feeling kinda proud. Denis was flabbergasted, pale

with anger. I let out a long stream of onomatopoeia and stashed the knife back in my crotch.

You are seriously ill in the head, you could have ruined everything.

I preferred it when Mr. Obesity stayed quiet, to be honest.

Watfh what you fay to me, you fucker. And ftop fquinting at me when you look at me! Your moronic little game iv up.

He banged on the table with his sausage fingers. *You're the moron, my squint is legit.*

Oh, I'm fo forry! But ftop infulting me or I fwear I'll kill you myfelf.

Denis cut our discussion short impatiently. *You're gonna tell us what you're doing here and who you're doing it for. We're in a rush.*

Nife and to the point, Denif.

He snorted. *Shut your face. And you, talk!*

Big Melon let it all out. *The Italians had me transferred here to monitor you. You messed up with Butterfly and—*

I did not meff up!

Well, you didn't close the file, and you snort more than you sell, your wing brings in next to nothing.

Denis turned from pale to translucent. He was being put in his place, and it was a place he was going to lose pretty soon.

I'm the one who's gonna take over once Big Dick is out of here. I still have twelve years on my sentence, I'll be doing some house-cleaning.

Denis was worried. He asked him what was going to happen to him, Big Dick's right-hand man, theoretically speaking the heir, the designated successor. Melon set him straight with a malicious little expression whose existence we hadn't even suspected a few minutes earlier. *You're gonna be working for Colossus!*

Poor Denis, he'd refused to hear me out. When you work in a team you have to be open to your colleagues' input. You have to pay for your mistakes; if you spit at heaven you shouldn't be surprised when God pisses on you.

I told you fo, I warned you!

Denis told me to shut up again. This last "shut up" turned out to be the straw that broke my very tolerant camel's back. While Melon was clarifying the situation, I'd had time to do a few calculations. When I was a Mafia henchman on the outside, I'd have more power than Denis would under Colossus and Melon on the inside.

I'd never have guessed that that very afternoon I'd find myself in isolation, accused of premeditated murder.

Right then, though, my criminal future looked bright. And I let rip with a violent burst of self-esteem.

You're the one who'v going to fut up, Denif! Fut up! Fut your fafe! Don't you ever tell me to fut up again! You fut up!

Denis was red now, bordering on purple. If it wasn't for the table between us, he'd have strangled me then and there. Melon cracked up laughing.

Fat Mireille and Paul showed up at our table. Melon switched from demonic laughter to moronic cackling. Denis relaxed his fists, but his face was still crimson. And I saved the day.

Forry, Melon wav getting on my nervev. I fouldn't have fouted at him.

As though I was a child being punished, Mireille ordered me to leave him in peace, adding that Melon couldn't defend himself, and told me to go back to my cell *immediately*. I obeyed with relief, since putting some distance between me and Denis seemed like an excellent idea.

From my cell, I could observe the table as the former senior executive negotiated his new working conditions with the former village idiot. The business world is an unstable organism. The way I was crouching also let me check that Tony was still stationed at the far end of the wing, and also allowed me to keep Edith in my sights.

Edith had her back to me and was chatting about me to Mireille. At least, that's what I guessed. Girls always talk about their love lives to each other, it's well documented. She must have been telling her how much she was suffering from this whole mess, and from that son of a bitch Jocelyn who had forbidden us, out of jealousy, to see each other. Talking about that kiss she'd refused me and now regretted.

Fat Mireille put a reassuring hand on her shoulder. *Love will find a way.* I was just speculating. With the same hand, she signalled something to the guard in the box. The noise of the door rang out. Mireille and Paul left, Tony vegetated, Edith unlocked the office door. It was the perfect moment. I only needed to walk a few steps. I turned to my colleagues one last time. Denis's defeated look communicated nothing but distress.

Fat Melon had somehow guessed that I was ready to act. He moved his massive bulk in my direction. His whole body was calling me to action. He shouted encouragement in his fat voice, making his three chins vibrate: *Go on! Go go go!*

It's crazy how much stuff can go through a feverish mind in four steps. *Remarkable*, as David Attenborough would say. He's the naturist who does animals on public television. Step one: I was going to make a name for myself as a fugitive. Step two: I'd show Melon and the Mafia I could wrap up a contract. Step three: I'd regain my freedom, settle my accounts on the outside, find my mother, reconcile with her, and then introduce her to my sweetheart. Because, step four: Edith and I would finally be able to love each other at long last. I was hella paved with good intentions.

My heart was thumping at top speed. Propelled by ambition, love, justice, and the four steps set out above, I jumped on Edith's back and yelled, *Watch out!* I pushed her against the half-open door, which her face hit, and then crushed her with a roar on the office floor. It was off to a good start.

18

PASSION

Edith was stunned. She stayed lying down when I got up to barricade the door behind us. *Hostage situation! Hostage situation!* Tony was yelling, being obliged to make a pretence of doing his job. I pushed the desk up against the door as the alarm went off. All this excitement was stressing me out. I was sweating like a pig from every pore of my body.

Edith struggled to turn around while I took the blade out of my pants. Her eyes widened in fear.

It'ƒ me! There'ƒ nothing to be afraid of.

I put her terrified look down to surprise. And maybe pain. She'd cut her forehead when she fell on the floor. And her chin. It was bleeding pretty good.

She stared at my knife, trembling all over. The phone rang. Already? This was all moving too fast, I needed some time to think and sort myself out.

Don't move, Edith! Don't move!

Between the alarm blaring and the phone ringing, I was having trouble concentrating. I needed to buy myself some time, ask them to call back in five minutes.

Call me back in five!

I slammed the phone down, but it just rang again. I turned to my sweetheart, who was even more stressed than I was, her body wracked with spasms, crouched in a corner in the fetal position.

You truft me, Edith, remember, I know you do, you told me fo yourfelf. I truft you av well…

I crouched down beside her, stroking her hair, trying to relax her.

Thif fank wav for you, I juft had to take you hoftave fo that Big Dick could efcape, but I'm going to do more than that. Do you underftand, Edith? I'm doing thif for you, for the two of uf, for love. Do you underftand?

Guessing my intentions, she burst into tears.

It'f all going to be okay, we're going to be together, juft the two of uf. I lay down next to her. She pressed up closer to the wall. I shifted closer and spooned with her. It was nice. Her hair smelled of soap. I hugged her hard so she'd stop trembling.

It'f going to be okay, Edith, pleave don't cry, I'm here for you. She stiffened, reassured. *Don't kill me!*

Girls are such romantics, always looking for drama.

Of courfe I won't! What are you faying? I'm leaving, but I'm not going to kill you. I'm taking you with me!

She cried harder. Now I was getting emotional. I wished this hug could go on forever, but we'd need to leave soon. It was getting to the crucial moment of giving orders to get Big Dick evacuated. Then I needed to get the doors opened for myself and escape with Edith. I really needed to focus.

I pressed my face into her hair, I clutched her to me and breathed her in. A little puff of courage. She held on to my arms, her nails digging into my skin, holding me back. She was afraid I was going to leave. The scent of her hair was intoxicating. I moved down toward her neck. At long last I could touch her skin, the soft, damp skin of her neck, salty on my tongue.

She tried to block my hands and keep them on her waist. Our desire was too strong. This wasn't the moment, but I followed her lead. It was hard to move my body, with her gripping my arms so passionately.

Relacf, bae, everything'f going to be fine.

I cupped her breast under the rough fabric of her shirt. My other hand rested on her crotch, on her work pants. She was panting and moaning.

No…no…

I know, Edith, thif ifn't the plafe. We fould ftop.

Yes, please stop!

But we were possessed by our desire. She wouldn't let me go and kept her nails dug into my flesh. My body could no longer wait to escape, to liberate itself. I couldn't wait anymore. We had to make love. Now. Make love just once, here, and then leave together.

As clumsy as the young lover that I was, I unbuttoned her shirt, using the knife to undo the big leather belt. It was like we were in a hardcore romance novel, both of us with tears in our eyes, awkward, seeming as though we were fighting in our clumsy attempts to take off the clothes that were stopping the marriage of our genitals. And our teeth kept bashing together in our rushed kisses. I was the gallant knight, covering her with a thousand kisses and smearing tears and blood over her face.

I was overjoyed to discover, with my exploring fingers, that her pussy was pretty tight. She'd waited for me: my lady love was still a virgin. I sucked my fingers and pushed my way inside her. She tensed up, twisted with fear, but I soothed her.

It'f normal to be nervouf the firft time. We'll take it flowly.

I didn't let myself get distracted by the ringing of the phone or by the prison alarm, nor by the negotiator who was bellowing into his megaphone. I simply savoured our bodies, united at last, after so much desire and waiting.

I focused attentively on our pleasure. Nothing else existed, not even the tactical police squad gathered behind the door as we orgasmed loudly, gasping with love.

When I opened my eyes again, I could only see her tears. Such happiness, such intensity. Was she crying with pleasure, satisfaction, love, or all of the above? I'd been a man for too long to cry wholeheartedly along with her. I had to take care of my responsibilities. Then they came to me, the only words—the only poem—worthy of the moment. *I love you.*

19

DETACHMENT

Butterfly was dead. Since the previous evening, Butterfly had been as dead as a dodo. There had been no chance of him coming out of his vegetative state, but he was in a stable condition and could have lived for decades with the hole in his neocortex. But his family had decided to donate his organs and pull the plug. In reverse order, luckily for Butterfly. It killed him. With a family like that, you'd be better off being an orphan.

But what did Butterfly have to lose by waiting around awhile? You never know with science: maybe researchers would have found a cure for comas. Tomorrow? In ten years? Who knows. Even Walt Disney thought it was worth taking a bet on cryogenics. But Butterfly's future died with him. His family killed him, but I'm the one who'll be found guilty. Another injustice to add to the list.

I've been rotting in the hole for more than six hours, with no food or water. The guards are depriving me of my fundamental rights. And the two officers from the SWAT team guarding the isolation cell don't reply to any of my demands. My lawyer gave me a bottle of water through the bean slot. I needed water to swallow everything they were telling me.

From the depths of the hole, I got hammered with the bad news, the tanker full of bad news. Bad news never comes singly, but this was like a birthday party at Octomom's house.

Big Dick is a fucking asshole. A rat. A snitch. He squealed on me. To protect himself, I'm guessing. When they strip-searched me, they found the instructions I was supposed to read, the details of his evacuation from the interior yard. They must have interrogated him right away. I mean, I guess it was partly my fault. But still, it's unbelievable, he broke the omertà code, the law of silence, the cornerstone of every self-respecting criminal organization. I thought he was one of the good ones. I feel hurt and disillusioned. You can't trust anyone, not even a notorious criminal. I should just be a gang of one.

If Big Dick had double-crossed me, then everyone else in the wing would do the same. So that left me in deep shit. The biggest surprises are often unexpected: not content to just grass me up for the attack on Butterfly, which ended up being a deferred murder, with a little help from his family, he was also denying all involvement in the hostage taking. That really takes the cake!

They were abandoning me again, and this was one time too many. If I'd drunk a drop of arsenic for every time I'd been betrayed, I'd have drowned a long time ago.

But I wouldn't go down alone! He thought he could fuck me over without any consequences? I'd screw him too, Big Fat Dick, right up his ass.

He denied being the author of the written demands they found on me. He even insisted he'd never spoken to me. The traitor! Like I'd just hallucinated the whole thing.

I'm a fcyhopath, fir, not fychotic! Let'f not get the two thingv micfed up!

My lawyer insisted I had to calm down, he couldn't stay and advise me if I was so agitated. How could you not be agitated if heaven and all its demons were falling on your head?

And I want to know how Edith'f doing.

You can't be serious, the lawyer said, shaking his head incredulously.

Of courfe I'm feriouf!

We'd just made love when they battered the door down like savages. I barely had time to stroke her hair and give her one last hug. Everything had been going so well, I could hear a chopper, I just needed to answer the phone, read the notes, leave the Italians a bit of time to get Big Dick out, then I'd start in with my own demands. And then it would be all wrapped up. There was no rush. They must have been imagining some bad shit on the other side of the door, thinking I was threatening Edith's life or something. They must have imagined the worst when I didn't answer the phone. But actually, the best was finally happening to me. Love at last.

This moment of grace was spoiled by those overexcited zealots from the SWAT team. The door, which had guarded our privacy, was ripped off its frame by a steel battering ram. It was like being in an extremely realistic video game. Helmeted and armed, spraying us with gas and yelling, an entire commando unit stormed the office. Flattened on the ground, I wasn't soaring anymore. Eeeeediiith! They took her away under my very eyes, crying hot tears. From the gas. And maybe from emotion too. Seconds later I was handcuffed, overpowered, on my back, gagged, and informed of my rights.

I was lifted off the ground by two workhorses armed to the hilt, and then dragged to the hole. Where I still am.

You'll be staying here until your court appearance on Monday.

The practical benefit of crimes committed in prison is that it saves on transport costs. This is no small saving for the good taxpayer.

We'll know more in court. For now, no news on Edith.

The lawyer guessed she was being supported by her team. The unit head had gone to the hospital with her, where she was probably going to be diagnosed with nervous shock.

Thofe baftardf traumatifed her, they didn't even give me a fhanfe to negofiate. They're barbarianv…

And I was sure Jocelyn was making the most of his chance to comfort her. There was no doubt about it, he'd be having a field day, taking advantage of my absence to tell her that I'd be convicted again, that it was no use waiting for me, and that she had no future with me. I punched the wall, fracturing a bone in my hand. *Oooowwww! Fuckety fuck!*

They're going to accuse you of premeditated murder, taking a hostage, illegal confinement, aggravated rape, and tutti quanti. My lawyer listed off the charges, shaking his head in discouragement. I didn't even know what a tutti quanti was, but I was sure I could defend myself on that count. The rape too. In all the commotion of the fighting, they'd spotted our lowered pants, and the fact that her face and both our genitals were bloody. I could see how it could be misunderstood. Edith would tell them that we were in a relationship and I hadn't raped her. My lawyer seemed pretty unconvinced. He was laying it on thicker than Marilyn Manson's foundation.

My valiant soldier of the law told me I could be added to the sex offenders registry. I couldn't see any advantages to that. It's basically just some professional guild, it's a group for people who like titles, and it protects the public more than it protects its members. I'd be challenging that too!

Things were looking bad for me. Very bad. He rattled off a litany of aggravating circumstances. He flopped theatrically into his chair and let out a weary sigh. He was playing the game, the poor sod. He was putting on these exasperated airs, but he seemed pretty happy about having all this on his plate.

I had nothing to eat until the next day. The guards were tormenting me. In the confusion after the hostage taking, they could claim they'd just forgotten. The bastards thought they were taking justice into their own hands. I took the fight to them and announced I was going on hunger strike. Ha!

I stared at the wall while I waited for my lawyer to visit again. I repeated the serenity prayer over and over, reminding myself that whatever happened, nothing could happen to me. I still had the essentials. The essentials are what's left when everything else has gone.

I had something stronger than justice, more powerful than the Mafia, more noble than the greatest reputation: I had love.

From my prone position on the floor, I stared miserably at the wall. I didn't know when I'd get anything to eat, or if I'd be transferred, or what revenge the underworld was planning against me, but I had love.

And underneath everything, here it was. Deep down inside my body, and carved into this wall forever: Edith and me, our initials scratched inside a heart. Forever.

EPILOGUE

Like a bonobo on ecstasy, Jocelyn must have jizzed happiness all over the prison. He'd managed to convince Edith to demand a permanent no-contact order for me. They even gave me back the thirteen letters full of poems I'd written her. The lawyer warned me to prepare myself psychologically: she could testify against me. They were messing with her head, those dirty sons of bitches.

And rumour had it there was a bounty on my head, nice and juicy, in the five-figure region. After everything I'd done for it, the Mafia was letting me down. I was tangled up in multiple family beefs. My life was in danger, and I was in danger of getting a life sentence.

But apparently all is not lost. My lawyer solemnly confided that he had a few precedents up his sleeve. *We can plead erotomania in the case of Ms. Edith Arsenault. As for Mr. Carol Quirion, alias Butterfly, we'll try legitimate defence. If not, we'll plead insanity for all charges, and then you'll be shipped off to the psychiatric hospital, but there won't be much chance of getting out of there.*

But I will get out. And quicker than you'd think. I have a mother and a wife to reunite with outside. I don't give a shit about your expertise and your rehabilitation. From now on, I'm only going to listen to my own conscience. Organized crime has fucked me over, too bad, so sad. I'll be a sole trader, and one day I'll trade their souls. With my mother and my woman at my side.

It doesn't matter where you lock me up, I'll escape. I'll escape and I'll get my revenge on all the people on my list. If you think I'm dangerous now, well, you ain't seen nothing yet.

But for now, I'm just hoping they'll send me to the psychiatric hospital. Prison's too crazy for me.

ACKNOWLEDGEMENTS

The author would like to thank Book*hug, Jay and Hazel Millar, JC Sutcliffe, Marie-Eve Gélinas, Carole Boutin, and all the inmates of the world for the inspiration. Read free or die!

The translator would like to thank David Goudreault, Marie-Eve Gelinas, Hazel Millar, Jay Millar, Stuart Ross, Malcolm Sutton, and Christopher Dummitt.

ABOUT THE AUTHOR

Marianne Deschênes

DAVID GOUDREAULT is a Quebecois novelist, poet, columnist and social worker. He has published three novels with Stanké, including *La Bête à sa mère* (*Mama's Boy*, Book*hug Press, 2018); *La Bête et sa cage* (*Mama's Boy Behind Bars*, Book*hug Press, 2019); and *Abattre la bête* (forthcoming in English from Book*hug Press in 2020). He has also published three poetry collections with Écrits des Forges. He was the first person from Quebec to win the Poetry World Cup in Paris (2011), and he has also received many other awards, including the Médaille de l'Assemblée Nationale (2012), the Prix des Nouvelles Voix de la Littérature (2016), the Prix de la ville de Sherbrooke (2016), the Grand Prix Littéraire Archambault (2016), and the Prix Lèvres Urbaines (2017). His work has been published internationally in France and Mexico. Goudreault lives in Sherbrooke, Quebec.

JC SUTCLIFFE is a writer, translator, book reviewer, and editor. She has translated several Quebec novels into English, including David Goudreault's *Mama's Boy*, *Document 1* by François Blais, and *Worst Case, We Get Married* by Sophie Bienvenu.

COLOPHON

Manufactured as the first English edition of
Mama's Boy Behind Bars
in the spring of 2019 by Book*hug Press.

Type + design by Tree Abraham
Copy edited by Stuart Ross

bookhugpress.ca